Truth or Dare

STONE
HALL
BOOKS

Other Books by Julie Coulter Bellon

Canadian Spies Series

Through Love's Trials

On the Edge

Time Will Tell

Doctors and Danger Series

All's Fair

Dangerous Connections

Ribbon of Darkness

Hostage Negotiation Team Series

All Fall Down (Hostage Negotiation Team #1)

Falling Slowly (Hostage Negotiation Team #1.5)

From the Ashes (Hostage Negotiation Team #2.5)

Pocket Full of Posies (Hostage Negotiation Team #3)

Forget Me Not (Hostage Negotiation Team #3.5)

Ring Around the Rosie (Hostage Negotiation Team #4)

Griffin Force Series

The Captive (Griffin Force #1)

The Captain (Griffin Force #2)

The Capture (Griffin Force #3)

Truth or Dare

A Novella

by

Julie Coulter Bellon

Copyright 2018 by Julie Coulter Bellon.

Published by Stone Hall Books.

Cover Design by Steven Novak Illustrations

Copyright 2018

ISBN-13: 978-0-9997946-2-3
ISBN-10: 0-9997946-2-0

Printed in the United States of America

First Printing September 2018

10   9   8   7   6   5   4   3   2   1

Acknowledgments

Thank you to Heather, Annette, Jon, and Robyn, who make my stories better and my life richer. And thank you to my family. I love you!

Chapter One

The spot where Jonah's foot should have been—had been until a year ago—was hurting again. The phantom pains from the amputation came mostly in the evenings now, which always made it hard to sleep. Jonah sat in the darkness of the family room, enjoying its black comfort, how it hid the display of track and field medals and trophies he'd won in high school. With the snowstorm that had been threatening all day finally unleashing itself, it was as if Mother Nature was commiserating with him. The howling wind outside perfectly matched his mood.

Good thing his parents weren't home to see this. His mother would frown and turn the lights on and offer to watch TV with him. Or she'd bustle around, getting him something to eat or wanting to know how he was feeling. That was the most dreaded question of all. He didn't know how he was feeling, but he did know he needed some peace and quiet.

Since coming home from rehab three days ago, this was the first evening he'd been alone. His friends and neighbors meant well, but there had been a steady stream of visitors to the house, coming to tell him how sorry they were for his "accident." As if losing his foot to a roadside bomb in Afghanistan was equivalent to a fender bender or something. But it was the pity in their eyes that bothered him the most. He didn't want anyone to pity him.

He leaned back in his father's recliner. His mother had instilled manners in him, so he'd smiled at everyone who came and tried to make it okay for them, but he'd never felt more alone. No one would ever understand what it was like to try to buy one shoe or have to put your pants on sitting down.

He flexed his good leg, careful not to hit the dog sleeping at his feet. Or really, just his foot. Jonah grimaced. Would he ever get used to only having one foot? Even after a year of rehab it didn't feel natural. Maybe it never would. His thoughts turned to the wine in the fridge. It would be so easy to numb himself, but going down that road never led anywhere good. He'd tried. It was time to get up and turn the lights on. Stop feeling sorry for himself and read a book or grab a movie to watch. Anything except more sitting in the dark.

Bending down to get his prosthetic foot, he pulled up the pant leg on his sweatpants, put the liner and sock over his stump, then strapped the prosthetic foot on and ratcheted it tight. "Wake up, Magnus." The golden retriever didn't even move. Jonah poked him gently in the side. "Hey."

Magnus's ears perked up, and he turned his face toward the door as if someone were there. "Just the wind, boy," Jonah assured him. "It's getting bad out there." But then he heard it, too. Something or someone was scratching at the back door.

Glad now that the lights were off, Jonah stood. If someone thought they could break into his house, they could think again. His military training kicked in, and he crept to the window. With the barest movement of the blinds, Jonah squinted to see the back porch through the swirling snow. It wasn't a human trying to break in, but a dog that wanted to come in.

He let out a breath, trying to calm the adrenaline running through his veins. "It's for you, Mag," he said, before he turned to flip on the lights.

His dog was standing in front of the door, pawing it. He obviously knew his visitor. Jonah walked over and opened it, letting in some snow and a smaller golden retriever who was obviously happy to see Magnus. She shook out the ice and snow from her fur, and Jonah watched, amused, as they greeted each other. "You've been holding out on me, buddy." He bent down to scratch her behind her ears. "And who do you belong to?"

She gave him a cursory glance before turning her attention back to Magnus. Jonah watched the dogs for a moment longer and then headed back to the recliner. They followed him and flopped down next to his chair when he sat down. The pair got comfortable lying next to each other. "A girl who likes a quiet evening at home? You're a lucky dog, Magnus."

The quiet didn't last long before the doorbell echoed through the house. Since he knew his parents had a key and he didn't expect them for another hour or so, Jonah thought about not answering it. But with the storm raging outside, he knew he had to let whoever it was in.

"Probably someone looking for your girlfriend," he said to Magnus as he got up from the chair. "At least I hope it is. Please don't let it be Ms. Davis." His mother's friend meant well, but when she'd come by earlier today she couldn't stop saying "you poor boy." It was enough to make any soldier want to go AWOL.

He walked slowly down the hall, grateful his parents didn't have stairs, or the person at the door would be waiting a lot longer. He opened it with both dogs at his heels. A woman stood in front of him, bundled in a parka, hat, and scarf so only her eyes were visible. She pulled her scarf down. "Hey, Jonah, I'm looking for my dog, Lola. Did she come over here?" She craned her neck, trying to get a look at the dogs who were hiding behind him.

Jonah was battling to hold the door with the wind and snow slamming into them so hard he could barely see the porch stairs. He motioned her inside. Once she was in, she pulled off her hat and scarf. Her short brown hair was sticking up at odd angles, but she didn't seem to care about anything except her dog.

"Lola, honey! You scared me! Never do that again." She hugged her dog while she scolded her. Magnus was trying to nose in on the hugging action, too, and got a scratch behind the ears for his trouble.

Jonah looked down at the reunion. She'd started to peel off her coat and gloves, while her dog danced around her. The woman's heart-shaped face dredged up memories from a lifetime ago.

Kami Jackson. A little zing of awareness skittered up his spine. Her smile was entwined with so many of his happiest high school memories. Being on the track team together. Star-gazing. Best friends for life. Or so he'd promised her. She'd matched him in humor, goals, and ambition, and he'd even allowed himself to imagine what it would be like to marry her. But after graduation, he'd joined the service, she'd fallen off the grid, and he'd had no choice but to let her go.

He swallowed, knowing he had to say something. "Hey, Kami."

She managed to look up at him while her dog finished bathing her chin. "We haven't seen each other in nearly six years, and all I get is a 'Hey, Kami?' Come on, you can do better than that."

Part of him wanted to smile at her sass, but he gave her an impassive stare instead. It would never be the same between them, so why try to go back? Besides, what did she want him to say? "Okay. How about, it looks like you need to get a leash for your dog."

She frowned up at him, and he saw the shadows under her eyes. She looked exhausted, and in that moment, he wished he'd said something to make her smile.

"I can see we're bothering you. I'll just take Lola and head home." She stood, and both dogs zigzagged around her legs, begging for more attention. "Just give me a second."

She tried to bend down and grab her gloves and got some more wet doggie kisses. Magnus was totally focused on her, but looked back at Jonah every now and then as if he couldn't understand why Jonah wasn't joining in on the fun. Would he even come to Jonah's side if he called? He wasn't sure. Magnus was giving Lola and Kami some pretty adoring looks, and it was obvious he knew them well. Jonah hadn't been a part of Magnus's life for a while.

He folded his arms, watching how easy it was for Kami to stay balanced while two dogs jumped on her. He'd always taken the ability to stand upright for granted. Watching her stand on two feet didn't hurt like it might have months ago, though. He'd worked really hard in rehab to deal with his feelings of loss and resentment, and he was grateful for that effort now.

Taking a breath, he watched her try to put her things back on and was surprised at how different she looked. The thin girl he remembered from high school was still trim, but her jeans and sweater now had curves in all the right places. Yet, her eyes that had always been laughing in high school, weren't laughing anymore. She had a hollow look in her face, like the people he'd seen visiting their loved ones at the rehab center. Did that have to do with losing her dog? Or seeing him? Probably the latter. Who wouldn't look like that, seeing him now?

He didn't wait to see the pity in her eyes or hear how sorry she was. Reaching for the handle, he opened the door and immediately felt a blast of cold. "I'm glad you found your dog."

Kami didn't say a word to Jonah, just snapped a leash on Lola's collar. The dog immediately sat down on her haunches in the doorway and began to whine when she looked outside. It did look pretty bad out there. The frigid wind effortlessly pushed the snow into drifts, blasting it sideways across the yard. Jonah turned in time to see Kami square her shoulders, her mouth pulled into a tight line.

He sighed inwardly. Okay, his mom had raised him better than this. He was out of line and that wasn't like him. The old him, anyway. "Hey, that storm's really picked up. Do you want to wait a bit and warm up at least?"

Even to him, his voice didn't sound very welcoming, and Kami's look of misgiving confirmed it. He was out of practice. Magnus stared up at him, clearly unimpressed at his attempt. The dog darted a glance at Kami as if to say, *yeah, my human's a little rusty at this. Sorry.*

Jonah straightened. His dog was not going to be embarrassed by his lack of manners. He could fix this.

Kami pulled on the leash. "No, thanks. We've bothered you enough. Come on, girl." She ducked her head, but not before he saw the hurt in her eyes. Guilt welled in him.

Jonah grabbed her arm as she squeezed by. "Hey, I'm sorry about what I said. Give me a chance to make it up to you." He bent down so she'd be forced to look at him. "I was just about to eat some of my mom's stew and that would definitely warm you up. Are you hungry?"

She hesitated, pinning him with her gaze as if to gauge his sincerity before she finally relented. "Okay, that would be great, actually." She didn't exactly look convinced as she took off her coat and gloves for the second time, but at least she'd agreed to stay.

When she turned, he could see her jeans were soaking wet.

How long was she looking for her dog? "You'll never get warm wearing that. I have some sweatpants you could borrow, and we could throw your jeans in the dryer."

She shivered and looked down. "Thanks. I'm freezing."

He was about to turn down the hall to his room, but his prosthetic foot caught on the rug in the entryway, and he stumbled. Biting back a curse, he put his hand on the wall to anchor himself and find his balance. He stood there for a moment, unwilling to meet her gaze. How could he limp along in front of the girl who remembered him as a confident track star? He didn't want her to see what he was now.

When he didn't move, she stepped forward. "Jonah?" Her cold fingers on his arm jolted him out of his thoughts.

He forced his feet to step forward, hoping all the gait training he'd suffered through to make his walk look normal had worked. "I'll be right back. You can wait in the kitchen. It's right through there."

She nodded and dropped her hand, as if she knew he didn't want to talk about it.

"Did you think I forgot where your kitchen is?" Kami gave him a small smile. Her voice was warmer now which helped Jonah to relax a bit. "It felt like we were either here at your house or at the track all through high school." She looked around and for just a second the exhaustion on her face melted away. "Don't you wish you could go back sometimes? Everything was so much simpler then."

Every day. Jonah still struggled to accept his new reality sometimes. It was too easy to wish for his life before the pain and rehab and managing a prosthetic. "We had some good times."

The brightness in her eyes faded. "Yeah, we did."

He waited until she'd started toward the kitchen before he walked down the hall to get the dry clothing for her. Magnus stood beside him and licked his hand. That dog still read him like a book. Jonah touched his silky head. "I'm all right, boy."

When he walked into the kitchen, Kami was on a stool, hunched over the island, her head in her hands. She looked small and defeated, something he'd never seen on her before. "You okay?" he asked as he joined her.

"Just tired." She tried to muster up a smile, but it looked more like a grimace.

"You still staying up late star-gazing?" He wanted to see a real smile on her face, one that reached her eyes.

"I wish." She looked down at her hands, folded in front of her. "Remember how hard I tried to teach you the constellations? You claimed you could never see them, but I always thought you could."

"I just wanted an excuse to stay out late." And to be near her. Even with her struggles in her home life she was light and fun, intelligent and driven, and that had drawn him to her. There had been so many times in their last year of high school that he'd thought about what it would be like if she were his girlfriend, but he didn't want to ruin the friendship if it didn't work out. In the end, he'd settled for staying best friends, but a part of him still wished he'd been braver and tried for something more. And if his reaction when he first saw her tonight was any clue, even after six years, those old feelings were still there for him. But so much had changed. Even if they did rekindle their relationship, what could he offer her now?

His tried and true friend-zone tactics he'd mastered when he was around her in high school kicked in and he stood to put some distance between them. "I'll warm up the stew and get the sugar cookies for dessert." He put his lead foot down carefully and walked slowly to the fridge.

"I love your mom's cookies. Did you decorate them?"

"She tried to get me to." It was a Christmas tradition at their house, and his reluctance had put a damper on it for his mom. His conscience twinged with guilt, remembering how he'd claimed he was tired and retreated to his room. He should have humored her.

"You were just trying to make sure they all stayed edible, I'm sure. You always did use way too much icing." Her sassy tone was coming back and he glanced back at her to see if she was smiling. From the way her lips were pressed together, Kami was barely holding back a grin. A little corner of his heart warmed to see it.

After carefully setting down the container of stew, he rested his palms on the counter, facing her. "Hey, I'm an expert at decorating those. And you can never have too much icing."

"When you can't tell if the cookie is supposed to be Santa or a stocking, there's too much icing." She quirked an eyebrow in challenge.

He shook his head. This was too easy. "Who cares what it's supposed to look like as long as it tastes good?"

She didn't admit defeat gracefully and merely rolled her eyes. "Because it's a sugar cookie, and decorating it to look like something is half of the fun."

"Mine look like something. Something good to eat." He leaned toward her. "You have to admit, I've got you there. I mean, what can you say to that? You know it's true because you finished off every cookie I ever brought you."

"How do you know I didn't give them to my dog?" Kami laughed and Lola pricked up her ears at her mistress, as if she was hoping for that very thing.

Jonah narrowed his eyes and pointed his finger toward her. "My cookies are a work of art. You just don't want to admit it."

She held up her hands in mock surrender. "Okay, okay, I'll plead the Fifth." She looked up at him and, for a moment, it was as if they were back in high school again with nothing more to worry about than next week's math test or tomorrow's track meet. But Kami dropped her eyes quickly and the moment was gone. She picked up the folded sweatpants from the counter. "Thanks again for letting me borrow these. I'll just go change out of my wet clothes before I say something that might incriminate me."

He chuckled as she disappeared into the guest bathroom. He couldn't remember the last time he'd joked around like that with someone. He'd missed it.

Turning toward the task at hand, he got things ready for their meal, getting out bowls and spoons. Before long, Jonah heard the bathroom door open and the dryer next to the mudroom start running.

When she came back into the kitchen, he noticed she'd smoothed her hair. It was strange not seeing her in the ponytail she'd worn through high school, but he could definitely get used to her short hair and how it drew attention to her eyes. As his gaze traveled downward to the sweatpants she'd borrowed, though, he could hardly smother a laugh. The waistband was pulled above her waist, and she'd rolled up the pant leg bottoms until it looked like she was wearing fat ankle weights.

"Let me guess. The pants didn't fit?"

She gave him her best are-you-kidding-me look. "Yeah, you're a bit taller than me." She turned her ankle to model the uneven rolls for him. "I might start a new fashion, though. Winter Storm

Chic. What do you think?"

"It could work." He gestured to the rolls. "And there's the feature of being able to pull the excess material down over your cold feet, which could be a selling point."

She shook her head. "I think someone already invented something for that. Called socks." She wiggled her bare toes.

"Do you need some? I've got extra." He inwardly winced. Of course with only one foot he'd have lots of extra socks, but he didn't want to call any attention to his injury if he could help it. Kami didn't even glance at his feet, though.

"I think I'm good, thanks." She moved past him and sat down on her stool at the kitchen island again. "So, is it weird being home?"

Here it comes. He'd wanted her to be different, but no one could resist fishing for gossip on how the town's amputee was doing. He glanced over at her, disappointed. "Not really."

But her face was still open and smiling. "It's all your dad was able to talk about. He's so glad you're here."

Jonah resisted the urge to stare at her. She didn't seem to be looking for gossip; she was just happy for him and his family. *When did I get so suspicious of people's motives?* "My dad loves to talk. Probably because his patients are captive audiences."

She laughed. "The perk of being a dentist, I guess."

"Is that where you saw my dad? At his office?" He rubbed his hand over his jaw. He wasn't surprised his dad had talked about him. His parents had been there for him through every step of his recovery, spending as much time with him as they could while he was at Walter Reed in Bethesda. When they'd asked him to come home to Hill Spring for Christmas, he couldn't say no.

"No." She shifted in her stool. "He came by the high school the other day with his sponsorship banner and we got to talk a bit." Then, as if she couldn't sit still, she slid off the stool and came to help him dish up the stew.

"He's sponsoring something?"

"Harrison Dental proudly supports the Hill Spring Huskies." She took the smaller bowl and headed for the microwave.

"Are you a sponsor, too?" He was trying to connect the dots, but something wasn't clicking. She'd always wanted to be an Olympic runner. What was she doing back in Hill Spring, anyway?

"I'm the new track coach at Hill Spring High."

"You replaced Coach Stubbs?" he asked.

She leaned in and he caught the faint, flowery scent of her shampoo. "Yeah, can you believe it? After thirty years of coaching, though, he can't leave it alone and still comes out to watch my practices."

Jonah had never thought that man would retire. Coach Stubbs lived and breathed the track team. He was the most intense man Jonah had ever met before he joined the Marines. Even then, he could only think of one or two drill sergeants that were more intense than Coach Stubbs. "That's got to be intimidating, having your old coach watch *you* be the coach."

"I keep thinking he's going to give me critique notes or something, but so far, he hasn't said a word. In a way, that's kind of worse. I mean, what if he hasn't said anything because he thinks I'm doing it all wrong?" She took the second bowl of stew from him and queued it up for the microwave.

"I'm sure you're doing great." And he meant it. She would be a great track coach.

He leaned against the counter and watched her punch in some numbers and press start to warm up the stew. Since the accident he'd always felt tense when he was in public or around people who weren't family, but that had evaporated with Kami. Their easy camaraderie had returned, as if they'd never been apart, and for the first time since he'd woken up in the hospital, he felt normal. But the best part was, there wasn't a trace of pity in her eyes when she talked to him.

He hadn't expected that, but he liked it. A lot.

Chapter Two

Kami kept her back turned as the microwave warmed the food. She needed to keep herself standing and busy, or she'd fall asleep. What a day this had been. One she never wanted to repeat. The nurses had forced her home for some rest, but then she'd realized Lola had gotten out somehow.

It seemed like everything that could have gone wrong today had.

But now that her panic at finding Lola missing was finally wearing off, her thoughts turned to memories of Jonah. Back in high school, he'd always been the rock that steadied and grounded her. And even now, with everything that had happened in the last seventy-two hours, she'd sorely needed his presence and hadn't even recognized it. Being here brought back so many warm memories for her, like sunshine chasing away all her shadows. The reality was, though some things seemed the same, their lives were very different than what they had been. She needed to keep that in mind.

Kami ran a hand through her damp hair and suppressed another shiver. She caught chills easily; that hadn't changed. Back in the day, no matter what season it was, Jonah would be hot and she'd always be cold. He usually had his arm around her to warm her up, though. That was one thing she wished hadn't changed, even if it was just for tonight.

She stole a peek behind her. The military had been good to Jonah. He'd always been athletic and good-looking, but now he was powerful and had a ruggedness to him. His blond hair was cropped, military-style, but the short-sleeved T-shirt he wore that proudly said *Marines* on it pulled across a broad chest and showed off some muscular arms. On the outside, he seemed more like his old self, but every now and then his change in demeanor told her he was struggling with some inner demons. She wasn't sure how to handle that. The Jonah she'd known had been so easy-going about most everything. She'd never seen him withdraw into himself before.

The microwave beeped and she pulled out the bowl and replaced it with the second one. *Turn around and face him; you're not some shy teenager. It's Jonah,* she scolded herself.

"So, have you done anything fun since you've gotten home? Been over to the Hill Spring Movie Festival yet? They're showing Christmas classics from the 30s and 40s this year with a live band playing carols in the lobby."

He watched her with such a serious look on his face, she couldn't help wishing he'd stayed easy to read. "No. I've been getting settled at home."

There it was again. The withdrawal. His voice sounded so flat, as if she shouldn't have even suggested he go out. *Maybe I shouldn't have. Maybe it's too hard for him to leave the house.* But he seemed to get around just fine. She shrugged. "Well, you probably had a lot of visitors. Once your dad let the cat out of the bag that you were coming home for Christmas, it spread like wildfire."

The microwave dinged, and she turned to pull out the last bowl. Pushing one in front of him and taking the other to her stool, she could feel his eyes on her. Nervous flutters started in her belly, and she couldn't sit next to him yet. Glancing around, she grabbed the kettle off the stove as if it was a lifeline and went to the sink to fill it. "If you have some hot chocolate mix, I can make us both a cup." She put it on to boil and took a breath before she came around the edge of the island to face him.

He was still watching her, and she couldn't read his expression. *Maybe I should have asked permission first. Maybe he hates hot chocolate now.*

"I don't have to, though, we could just eat," she said, turning to take the kettle off. He wasn't saying anything, and she didn't know what to do anymore. Her mind and body were just too tired to figure it out.

He reached across the island and held her arm. Even though his touch was light, tingles raced up her shoulder and down her spine. "Hot chocolate would be great, thanks."

Her breath caught as she met his gaze, and all her tiredness fled. After all these years, he could still affect her like this. He definitely didn't have the same outgoing personality he'd had in high school, though. There was a lot going on behind those blue eyes, and he didn't seem in the mood to share. Not that she would ask him to. She could hardly imagine what he'd been through in the last year, and her heart ached.

Jonah took a step toward her and sat down. The truth was if she didn't know he'd lost a foot, she wouldn't have guessed it. His limp was hardly noticeable and he moved well. He must have had a fantastic physical therapist. But from his frosty reception when she'd first arrived, she didn't want to bring up any uncomfortable topics.

He seemed to be on the same wavelength. "So, how did this doggie romance get started?" he asked before he took a bite. She smiled. The dogs were a pretty safe topic to talk about.

"I'm not sure. She's been sneaking out the past few nights and making visits to dogs she's met at the park." She was grateful that her neighbors had caught her, since Kami had been watching over Ben in the hospital. She touched the bridge of her nose, pushing those thoughts away for the moment. "I can't figure out how she's getting out. I might start calling her Houdini. I can't even tell you how relieved I was that she was over here and safe with that storm outside."

They both looked at the dogs, who were sitting at attention and staring at them. Or staring at the stew in their bowls.

"Magnus, you know Mom would kill me if I gave you any of her stew," Jonah admonished with a shake of his head. "You have plenty of food in your dish." Magnus gave him a soulful stare. "All right." He got up and moved to the cupboard, taking a box of dog treats out. "Here's a little something for you and your lady friend."

The dogs settled down with their treats, and Jonah talked to them the entire time about being good dogs. Kami tore her eyes away from the scene. He was adorable with the animals, like he'd always been, and it made her heart melt. Even something as devastating as losing a limb hadn't taken the sweetness out of him. She rubbed her eyes. Being so tired was making her sentimental. Thankfully the kettle whistled and gave her something to do besides stare at the man next to her.

"The box of hot chocolate packets is in the pantry, first shelf on the left."

"Thanks." She concentrated on getting the hot chocolate ready, worried that it would be lumpy. Somehow hers was always lumpy no matter what she did, but Ben never minded. She felt the sting of tears and quickly blinked them away. Bending over her task, she hoped Jonah hadn't noticed. Stirring the lumps out of that hot chocolate became her new mission in life until she could get a handle on herself and her emotions. She finally handed him a cup of non-lumpy hot chocolate, a triumphant smile on her face. He gave her a funny look.

Do I look teary? She made her smile bigger, but that just made him frown. *For Pete's sake, don't scare the man.*

"Thanks."

He was watching her too closely, so she backed away. Kami sat down and finally concentrated on taking a bite of her stew. It smelled divine and reminded her that she hadn't had a chance to eat much today. "This is so good." She took several more bites, the warmth of the food taking the edge off the cold.

Jonah raised his eyebrows at her nearly empty bowl. "You were really hungry."

"I didn't have time to eat and I really hate—" She stopped herself. She'd almost said hospital cafeteria food. That was a subject she didn't want to broach with him, not if she didn't want to dissolve into tears. Besides, he probably didn't want to talk about hospitals anyway, with what he'd been through in the last twelve months. And all she could think about was Ben being there when he should be home safe with her.

She felt the prickle of tears again and forced her thoughts to

Jonah and high school. It had been such a happy time for her, filled with so many hopes and big dreams with nothing but smiles for the future she'd planned. But she wasn't that girl anymore, and that wasn't her life. Part of her wished it were, though. She couldn't control the little sigh that escaped for what might have been.

"You really hate . . . what?" He leaned forward on his elbows, giving her his full attention.

She pulled her thoughts back to the conversation. "I, uh, really hate it when that happens." She wanted to slap her hand against her forehead. She sounded like an idiot, but she couldn't talk about Ben. Or hospitals. Or anything that would make her cry. She wanted to be the girl Jonah remembered, someone who could handle whatever life threw at her.

Jonah leaned back, giving her a little more space. "I know it's been awhile, but I still know you, and something's wrong." He reached for her hand, and she let him take it. "If you want to talk about it, I'm here."

Tears filled her eyes, and she swallowed hard. It had been so long since she'd had someone to lean on and confide in. Six years, to be exact. And he was still so perceptive when it came to her and her feelings. She looked down, blinking away her tears. She was not going to cry in front of him if she could help it, and that effort made her throat too tight to talk. Kami squeezed his fingers before she stood and took her bowl to the sink. Taking a second to gather herself, she rinsed it out slowly. Finally, she turned around and found her voice. "It's a long story."

He lifted a hand. "We've got time. And some hot chocolate. I'll even make a fire if you like. Just like old times."

No, it wouldn't be like old times. Back then, they'd sit in front of his fireplace and talk about running strategies and if the team had a chance to go to state. If she sat there with him tonight, she'd have to tell him why she'd never achieved any of her goals. She'd have to tell him about Ben. Could she really lay her soul bare to Jonah? Could she look into his eyes and see the disappointment that was sure to be there?

As if the universe had heard her thoughts and wanted to help, the lights flickered out. But if anything, her anxiety only grew. How would Jonah feel about her if he knew the truth?

Chapter Three

As soon as the lights went out, Jonah grabbed the counter, feeling the dogs brush against his legs. Falling in front of Kami was the last thing he needed. At least it was dark if he did. "Let me get a flashlight."

Hopefully his mother still kept them above the fridge. He moved slowly, pushing the dogs out of the way with his prosthetic. Opening the cupboard and feeling his way inside, he was grateful to touch the shape of a flashlight in the corner. He flipped it on, careful not to shine it in her face. "Good thing we ate before we lost power."

"Too bad about my pants in the dryer, though. I might have to wear yours home." She bit her lip. "Do you think your parents are okay?"

"The staff Christmas party is at the hotel ballroom so if the storm is too bad, I'm sure they'll just book a room at the hotel for the night. Although knowing my mother, she'll plow through the storm in her heels to make sure I'm not alone."

Kami made a noise of commiseration. "It's hard for her not to baby you, I imagine, but it's only because she loves you."

"I know. I haven't exactly gone easy on her." He thought back to his mom's excited invitation to go with them to the Hill Spring Movie Festival and how her face fell when he said no. He didn't want people gawking at him, but he could have let her down easy. He should have. "I'm lucky to have her."

"Yes, you are," Kami said quietly. "I can only imagine how she feels having you home safe and sound."

He could hear the hitch in her voice. There was definitely something else going on with her, but he didn't push. For now.

Jonah opened the drawer next to him and picked up some matches. "Should we go into the family room? You can get your pants and dry them in there. I really can start a fire."

He offered her the flashlight, and she took it. "That sounds great." She got her jeans out of the silent dryer and dragged in a kitchen chair to drape them over next to the fireplace. She walked back and handed him the flashlight when she was done. "I'm definitely ready for that fire."

A sense of satisfaction went through him that she didn't question whether he could do it. The fact was, he hadn't done much for himself since he'd come home and definitely hadn't taken care of anyone for longer than he cared to remember. He grabbed his mug, feeling lucky. Sure, he was walking slowly, but he was balanced and hadn't fallen on his face so far.

She followed behind with her mug and sat in his father's recliner, which was closest to the fireplace, rolling the bottom of the sweatpants over her feet with one hand. "I just can't get warm."

Jonah knelt down and pulled back the fireplace screen. "Just give me a minute."

Before long he had a roaring fire going and he sat back, pleased with himself—until he realized that getting back up on his feet was going to be awkward, especially in front of her. Those old feelings of frustration came rushing back and his fists clenched involuntarily. He didn't want to make a fool of himself or have her see him struggle. So the obvious solution was to just sit here on the floor. Watching over the fire was the perfect excuse.

He looked up at her, but she hadn't even noticed his moment of indecision. She was clutching her mug of hot chocolate as if it were a lifeline, a little shiver running over her. In the old days, he would have pulled her close against him to warm her up, but that might be awkward now. Jonah reached back and grabbed the blanket off the arm of the couch. "Here. This should help."

"Thanks," she said, sliding to the floor beside him as she took it. "Maybe I'll just get closer to the fire."

He moved back a little to make room for her, and the two

dogs joined them, snuggling at Kami's feet, as if they knew she needed their body heat. With only the firelight to illuminate the room, her face was shadowed now, and the exhaustion lines were back. He really wanted to know what was going on with her, but knew he had to be patient. He'd worked hard in high school to get her to open up about her home life and why her parents never came to their track meets. Back then, she'd been so independent and didn't trust easily. Surely she knew he would still keep her secrets.

Maybe this is about her mom again. Was she in rehab finally? He shifted slightly. That wasn't an easy topic to bring up, so he stuck to the dogs, nodding toward their sleeping forms, practically draping themselves across her legs. "Well, if you can't get warm with those two beside you, nothing will help."

Magnus raised his head and gave Jonah a sleepy look. "Hey," he said to Magnus. "You just going to leave me over here in the cold?" Magnus gave him a *"sorry, buddy"* look and lay back down with a yawn. "Wow," Jonah said, shaking his head.

Kami laughed. "Those two are pretty inseparable. I hadn't realized it was so serious already."

He liked the sound of her laugh and was glad it hadn't changed. "Magnus didn't even mention he was seeing anyone, and here I thought we told each other everything."

With the dogs, the fire, and the two of them so close together, it was as if there was a little cocoon around them where the world, and its pain couldn't enter. He let out a deep breath and relaxed. Picking up his mug, he slowly drank a bit of his hot chocolate. *So smooth.* Whenever he made it from a powder he could never get the lumps out. She obviously had refined her hot chocolate talent.

He watched her, that hollowness back in her eyes, and he had to ask her again. "So, I think you were just going to tell me a long story about what's going on with you."

She fingered the edge of the blanket. "Since we're re-creating old times, let's play our game."

Our game.

The words echoed in his head, and his stomach tightened. Their game was truth or dare. He'd never turned down her dares before, and she'd given him some crazy ones. What if he couldn't do it now? And what if her "truth" questions were about his injury?

Everyone had been dancing around his missing foot since he'd been hurt. How did it happen? How are you feeling? He hated talking about it. He didn't want to relive the day, and he didn't know how he was feeling half the time. Jonah tamped down a sigh. The world just couldn't let him have one moment of peace. But when he looked up at her to see her eyes watching him so intently over the rim of her mug, he knew he'd try. If that was the price of letting her know she could still trust him, he'd pay it. Besides, what else were they going to do until the lights came back on?

"Okay."

She laughed again. "You don't sound very sure. I'll go easy on you."

"Promise?" *Can she see that word for the plea it is?* "I'll take truth."

"What did you get your parents for Christmas this year?" She tilted her head. "See? Easy."

But Jonah inwardly jolted at the question. He hadn't gotten his parents anything yet. But since Christmas was a week away, he should have. "I'm still thinking about what they'd like." The excuse rang empty to his ears, but Kami didn't seem to notice.

"At my last dental checkup your dad confessed to me how much he loves *Doctor Who*, so I made him a *Doctor Who* scarf." She gave him a sly grin. "I got your mom the *Pride and Prejudice* with Colin Firth in it so she has something fun to watch, too. Because, you know, Colin Firth."

Jonah watched her, liking how happy she was. This was the girl he remembered, happy, giving, and a little mischievous. Obviously the woman she'd become had some secrets. But that could wait a little longer.

The matter at hand was, how did he not know his dad was into *Doctor Who*? "So you're a knitter? That surprises me. How can you sit still for that long?"

She lightly smacked his arm. "You're one to talk. You could

never sit still."

"Actually, I do a lot of sitting these days." And just like that, the happy mood was gone.

"You don't have to," she said quietly. "Looks to me like you're doing great."

How could he explain what it was like to lose a limb, to learn to walk again, the pain? He couldn't and didn't want to. But with a year of recovery behind him, he knew she was right. He was doing great and he needed to acknowledge that more. "You're still bossy." But when he looked at her face, so familiar, yet different, he saw a strength around her now. Did she see that when she looked in the mirror?

"I prefer to think of it as helpful."

"Well, maybe I should sit just a little longer so I can at least have a *Doctor Who* marathon and catch up with my dad." He nudged her shoulder. "If that's okay with you."

She quirked up her lips into a half-smile and Jonah smiled with her. The happy mood was back. How long had it been since he'd been this relaxed with another human being? He honestly couldn't remember.

"I don't watch it myself, but almost everyone at work loves it." She took another sip of hot chocolate. "Maybe you could invite me over to your marathon. I'd even bring Lola for Magnus."

"Sounds great." And he meant it. He wouldn't mind

spending more time with her. "So, my turn, right?"

"I pick truth."

He let out a breath, glad she hadn't said dare. He didn't want to dare her to do anything because then she'd get him back on her next turn. "What's the best part of your job?"

"The kids." She ran a hand through her hair, making it stand up again. "I love pushing them and seeing them improve. It's a rush."

"So you relate to Coach Stubbs then?" He crossed his legs under him while he waited for her answer.

"Yes and no. I loved Coach, but he pushed too hard sometimes. I work to make sure I don't cross that line, that the kids stay motivated and encouraged."

Jonah nodded. "I always felt like I'd let him down if I didn't place."

"Yeah. Me, too. Which is good and bad for a kid, you know?" She set down her mug and began petting Lola's head. "I want them to do better than they did last time. To keep trying and never give up. That's what I want them to remember when they think of me." She looked over at him, and he could see a flush on her cheeks. "Sorry, I sound like a motivational speaker or something."

"Don't worry, I've heard them all." He leaned closer. "And you're a lot prettier than the ones I had." Her flush deepened, and he grinned. "Do you still run?"

"I get in a few miles a day, and there's at least one kid who likes to challenge me at practice," she admitted. "I can hold my own."

Of that Jonah had no doubt. "You were pretty good in high school."

"Pretty good? I seem to recall beating your times more than once." She lifted her chin.

He held his hands up in mock surrender. "All right, you were awesome."

Kami rolled her eyes. "Okay, my turn. With two 'truths' out of the way, you know what it's time for. Dares."

She looked around the room for something to dare him with, and Jonah's heart sank. "There's not much we can do in the dark. What about another truth?" He hoped he didn't sound as anxious as he thought he did.

Her gaze swung back to him, and she raised her eyebrows. "Are you chicken?"

Yes.

But he didn't want to admit how scared he really was, to somehow still be the guy she remembered. There was a chance he could fall or embarrass himself. Or wouldn't be able to do what she asked at all. But the alternative was to chicken out, and that was unacceptable. He pushed down his insecurities. He was Jonah Harrison, and he could do this. "Okay, what's your dare?"

She held out her mug and gave him a steady stare. "Get us refills."

Jonah stiffened. Why would she ask that? Did she think he couldn't do something so simple? Or was he overthinking it? He sighed inwardly, wavering, trying to keep things light just in case. "You just want to sit here warm by the fire while I serve you."

"You got me." Her smile reached all the way to her eyes this time. "Do you accept the dare or not?"

He'd come too far to back down now. "Of course."

His voice was nonchalant, but his hands were already starting to sweat. He got on his knees and pushed himself up. After a little hop for balance, he was standing. Holding two mugs by the handles in one hand and a flashlight in the other, he headed for the kitchen. He could feel her eyes on him, but he moved slowly and deliberately. No way was he going to screw this up. Jonah had always given dares his best effort, from eating a rose to giving himself a haircut. He wasn't going to give any less now, prosthetic foot or not.

Chapter Four

Kami couldn't see Jonah's face, but she could feel his determination as he slowly walked across the room. In the darkness she watched his shadow and could see and hear a small shuffle in between his steps.

Is his prosthetic bothering him? It was easy to see he didn't want to do it, but she was proud of him for taking the dare. Maybe he was afraid he'd fall in front of her or something. For a second, she thought he might refuse to do it at all, but then he'd clenched his jaw and done it, just as she knew he could. Pride swelled in her heart. Jonah had always been innately sure of himself and what he could do. His injury might have hidden that from him, but hadn't destroyed it completely. In the brief second after he'd accepted her dare, she'd seen it in his eyes again.

When he returned and drew close to the fire with that little hesitation in his step, she could see how hard he was concentrating on not spilling the hot chocolate. She wanted to say how proud she was, but knew instinctively that wouldn't go over well so she stayed silent, focusing on the steam coming from the mugs. Gooseflesh prickled on her arms and she rubbed her hands over them. The fire and the dogs hadn't been able to completely ward off the chill she'd gotten looking for Lola in the snowstorm, and she was really looking forward to something hot.

"Thanks," she murmured as she took the drink from him. She needed it to warm her from the inside, but wished she could wrap her whole body around the warmth of the mug.

Jonah set his own drink on the hearth and sank down heavily in front of her. She watched him as he grabbed the poker to stoke the fire. He looked pleased with himself, and a frisson of happiness caught in her chest. *He did it, and he's as proud as I am.*

"Are you warming up yet?" He sat back, his hands hanging over his knees, his ever-watchful eyes missing nothing.

"Not really." Even as she said it another shiver raced through her. "Probably just caught a little chill. The hot chocolate will help in a minute."

He tilted his head down and then raised it to look her in the eye. "It's my turn, right?"

Kami nodded, her stomach flipping at the intensity in his face. "Yep."

Suddenly the room seemed very small. This dare sounded

serious. He'd dared her to do some pretty crazy things in the past, but they'd been kids then. From the tone of his voice, whatever he was going to ask was way above wearing a clown nose to a restaurant or singing "Yankee Doodle" at the top of her lungs on a street corner.

"Just to be fair, I'm going to ask, truth or dare?" He was holding himself still, but there was an energy zinging between them that made her antsy.

She took a breath. "You know I have to take the dare if we're using our old rules."

His gaze never left hers and he didn't hesitate. "I dare you to let me help warm you up."

Several scenarios from the past raced through her mind. He used to let her warm up by putting his arm around her and holding her close to his side. Was that what he was thinking? Or did he mean get her another blanket?

"What did you have in mind?" Her pulse rate picked up as she thought about what she wanted him to say.

He grinned and shook his head slightly, as if he could read her thoughts. Kami flushed and hoped he couldn't see it in the dark.

"Before you go thinking my intentions are anything but honorable, I just thought that sharing body heat could help warm you up faster." He held out his arms. "Just snuggle your back against me and with the blanket over us, you'll be warm in no time."

Her shivering body wouldn't allow her to say no even if she'd wanted to, which she didn't. "Okay."

Her heart hammered as she scooted over between his knees, her back against his chest. Curling the blanket around them, she practically melted into him. "How are you always so warm?" she murmured.

He ran his hands up her arms, leaving a trail of heat behind them. "How are you always so cold?" Wrapping his arms around her, he tucked her closer against him.

Kami closed her eyes, her cheek against his chest, breathing in his clean laundry scent. Being in his arms was like coming home after an extended trip. All the fear and anxiety she'd been dealing with were suddenly far away. His heartbeat was in her ear, sure and steady, like him. It would be so easy to fall asleep if her thoughts hadn't turned to how close his mouth was.

What would it be like to kiss him? She shifted in his arms, moving closer, grateful he couldn't read her thoughts.

He rested his chin on the crown of her head, his hands still moving slowly up and down her arms. "I need to figure out a harder dare next time. I didn't even have to say it twice."

"I know a good thing when I hear it." She didn't want to move as his body heat began to chip away at the ice in her veins. "You ready? It's my turn."

"Well, since we just got comfortable, I pick truth."

Kami looked at the flames crackling next to them. Did she dare ask it? "What's your biggest regret since you came home from Afghanistan?"

His hands stilled and silence followed the question. "I should have picked dare," he muttered.

She wanted to take back her words so she didn't spoil what was building between them. "Never mind. You don't have to answer that."

"No, I want to." His arms tightened around her middle. "It's not that easy to explain. The longer I sit here with you, the more regrets I have."

His words pricked her heart. She'd thought things were going so well, that he was okay with her being here. Maybe she'd pushed him too far. Or maybe he had more demons to work through than she thought.

Kami shrank back a little. "I'm sorry. I didn't mean—"

"No, no, that came out wrong. I just..." His words trailed off. "I look at you knitting a scarf for my dad and getting girl movies for my mom, and if I'm honest with myself, I've been pretty selfish over the past year."

"You went through something life-changing," she said softly, turning in his arms so they could see each other. "You're allowed to be selfish. Sometimes things happen that take us in a completely different direction." Ben popped into her mind. She'd sacrificed so much for him, but she'd do it all over again.

"You sound like you're speaking from experience." He took one of her hands, rubbing his thumb over the back of it. "Care to share?"

"Hey, this is my turn to ask the question. You have to wait." She knew his questions were coming, but didn't mind putting it off a bit longer. "And for future reference, *Pride and Prejudice* isn't just a girl movie, you know."

He gave her a *"yeah right"* look. "Definitely a girly movie."

"Just because I didn't want to hurt your feelings on the cookie argument doesn't mean I'll let you get away with that kind of statement. Have you watched it?" His silence confirmed her suspicion. "You do realize the entire movie is about judging someone before you get to know them?"

"I don't need to watch it. Colin Firth is in it." He raised his eyebrow. "You said so yourself."

"That doesn't mean anything. The man is an amazing actor who's been in a lot of movies. If you don't want to see the one with Colin Firth in it, you can see the one with Kiera Knightley. I think you'd like that one. And both of them have tons of fantastic dialogue."

Jonah groaned. "Dialogue? Are there any explosions? Swordfights? An awesome bad guy?"

Kami nodded her head. "Mr. Wickham does some terrible things."

He made a face like he'd smelled something terrible. "Okay, he can't be an awesome bad guy with Wickham for a name. It's definitely a girly movie."

"No judgments until you've watched it," she said firmly.

"You're being bossy again, but I'll concede on this one until I've watched the show." He touched her back and started rubbing slow lazy circles around the center. "So, the answer to your truth or dare question is, I regret being selfish and," he gave a loud sigh, "maybe a little judgmental about *Pride and Prejudice*."

It was getting harder to breathe, her heart tripping over itself the more his fingers moved over her back, leaving a trail of awareness wherever he touched.

"You were dealing with something no one should have to deal with," Kami said finally, leaning against his chest so he couldn't have access to her back anymore. "No one faults you for being wrapped up in your recovery."

"I know. But I could have been a little more grateful for my parents. A little more upbeat when my buddies called. And a little more welcoming to you." This time he squeezed her in a hug. "I'm sorry."

His touch had started a firestorm inside of her that was warming her up from the inside better than a dozen cups of hot

41

chocolate. "Apology accepted."

She looked up at him and he leaned down. Their lips were only millimeters apart. Was he going to kiss her? Did she want him to?

"I think it's your turn." Her voice sounded breathless to her ears. "I pick truth."

The corner of his mouth lifted as if he was trying to hold back a grin. Could he read her thoughts? Was she wrong? His thumb ran over her shoulder in a slow circuit that calmed her racing thoughts.

"Okay. Why are you still in Hill Spring? I thought you wanted to leave and be an Olympic runner." His voice was quiet, but the question was like cold water on her head.

She'd known it was coming, but it was still hard. She closed her eyes. Once upon a time, her Olympic dreams had been everything to her. How could she explain and see the look on his face? She couldn't bear his disappointment.

"Like I said, it's a very long story." She pulled the blanket closer around her. The fire and their closeness had made her feel safe, but now all the emotions she'd been holding in came rushing to the surface. Anxiety surged over her like a tidal wave.

His hands stilled on her shoulders. "You can trust me, Kam."

"I know." She pushed her hair back behind her ear and fixed her gaze on her sleeping dog, finding it easier to talk if she wasn't looking at Jonah. "I've always trusted you."

Gathering her courage, she took his hand. "And I want to tell you about Ben."

Chapter Five

Jonah's heart rate picked up. Who was Ben? Her husband? Her son? *Is he why she didn't keep in touch with me after high school?* Whoever he was, he was obviously difficult for her to talk about. She'd practically curled into a ball on his lap.

She took a deep breath and let it out before she spoke. "Just after our high school graduation, my little sister found out she was expecting a baby."

Jonah remembered Hailey. Really social, not really concerned about classes. The opposite of Kami.

"With no father in the picture and my mom in rehab again for her drug abuse, Hailey had no one to turn to, so I stepped in." The room was so quiet, he couldn't even hear the dogs snoring anymore. He didn't break the silence, just held her hand and waited for her to continue.

"I gave up my track scholarship to Stanford and went to community college so Hailey could get her GED before the baby came, and I don't regret it." Her hands clenched as if she thought he would second-guess her decision.

"Why would you regret it?" He was genuinely confused.

"I don't want you to be disappointed in me." She threw up a hand. "At first, I was so busy helping Hailey that I didn't have time to answer your emails, but then when I heard how well you were doing, I didn't want you to be disappointed with how things turned out for me." Dropping her chin to her chest she said softly, "I told you I was getting out of here, away from my mom and all my family's problems. That I was starting over. But I let it all go in a heartbeat."

Jonah turned her in his arms so she would see him. Hear him. "You said you wouldn't let your mom's addictions hold you back. And you didn't. How could I be disappointed in that? Look at what you've accomplished. You helped your sister become a mother at a really young age and you were hardly older than she was. And yet you got your own degree and have a teaching job doing something you love." A tear rolled down her cheek, and he wiped it away with his thumb. "You've always been so strong. I can't even imagine how hard it was for you. I'm not disappointed; I'm proud."

She sniffed. "I didn't feel strong. The past six years have been hard, but Ben makes it all worth it."

"Tell me about him." He wanted to know everything and

wished he would have tried harder to keep in contact with her all those years ago. He should have known something was happening in her life preventing her from answering his emails.

Her face lit up as soon as she started talking. "Ben's amazing. He was the most cuddly baby and filled all the empty places in my heart the moment I held him in my arms. He just started kindergarten this year, and he's so smart. When he stayed with me for track practice, the kids loved him." She brushed away another tear. "Ben is our world."

Something had happened to Ben. Jonah knew it was coming and part of him didn't want her to say it out loud. She'd already had so much heartache in her life with a single mom addicted to painkillers, and now she'd given up her dreams to help her sister be a single mom. If anyone deserved a break, Kami did. But she needed to get it out and he wanted to be the person to help her get through it. Whatever *it* was. "You can tell me, Kam."

She closed her eyes. "They were in a car accident three days ago. I've been at their bedside until tonight, when the nurses made me go home to get some rest."

Jonah tightened his arms around her, feeling the tension in her body and wishing he could take some of it away from her. "Are they going to be okay?"

"My sister has a broken pelvis and several broken ribs. Her face is pretty swollen." She turned her face into his chest and he held it there, his hands stroking her hair.

"What about Ben?"

She swallowed hard. "Thankfully he was buckled in his car seat, but even with that, he broke some ribs and his arm. It's the head injury we're all worried about." Her voice was hoarse and uneven. It was obvious she was near her breaking point.

Jonah went very still. "He'll get better, right?"

"They're watching him closely, but the doctor thinks so. It's just going to take some time. Ben was sleeping when I left, but there were so many tubes and machines around him." This time she buried her face in his shirt and let the tears come. "I could have lost them both."

"Shh... You didn't. He's going to be fine." Jonah continued stroking her hair to soothe her. When the tears subsided, he turned her chin so he could see her face. "*You're* going to be fine."

She brushed at his shirt. "I'm sorry I cried all over you."

He pulled her back against him. "I'm not sorry at all." She lay against his chest again, the emotion taking any energy she'd had. They sat there quietly, listening to the storm outside and the fire crackling beside them. Sitting in the dark with her as a teen, usually staring at constellations in the sky, had been a cherished memory for him even after they'd lost contact. But now he'd found her again, and he knew this night was one he'd think about for years to come.

"Kam, I spent a lot of time in the hospital, and the holidays were the worst. I can't imagine being a little kid in the hospital at Christmastime. Do you think we could visit Ben together? Maybe bring some Christmas presents?" Jonah asked softly, not wanting to break the peaceful stillness surrounding them. Even the storm outside seemed calmer now. "If you think it's a good idea, of course."

He surprised himself with the offer, but it felt right. He didn't know Ben, and he hadn't gone out of his house since he'd gotten home, but he felt a bond with the little guy already. Especially knowing how important he was to Kami.

"That would be great." Kami tilted her head back to look at him. "I know he'd love to hear all about your time in the Marines. He wants to be Captain America when he grows up, and that's pretty close."

It really wasn't, but he wouldn't tell her that. The long, dusty patrols far away in Afghanistan had made him appreciate everything he'd had at home. "I'd like that," he said. "Captain America toys are at the top of our Christmas list for Ben then."

They settled down again, watching the flames in the fireplace. She seemed lighter somehow, as if telling him had relieved her of a heavy burden. He ran a hand up her arm, wishing his presence could always take her troubles away.

Just like she's done for me. He hadn't even thought about his own pain since she'd been in his arms. It was amazing how much less his own foot bothered him when he was talking about her problems and planning a hospital visit. Not that he was pain-free or anything. He was itching to take off his prosthesis. But, for now, just being with her was enough.

He picked up his mug, careful to still keep her close, and finished off the hot chocolate. "Does this mean the game's over?"

She shook her head. "Not when it's my turn."

He groaned. "Just remember I was nice to you last time we did dares."

And nice to myself. It felt right having her so close.

She laid her hands on his forearms, as if bracing him for what she was about to say. "This one is sort of a truth *and* a dare."

He tensed. That didn't sound good.

She let the blanket fall to her waist as she met his eyes. "Jonah, I've noticed you've been rubbing your leg and shifting around. If you need to take your prosthetic off, you should do it."

She was perceptive, he'd give her that. And he wasn't as good at hiding his discomfort as he thought he was. "Normally I would have taken it off by now," he confessed.

"Are you afraid to do it because I'm here?" She leaned closer. "I know it must be hard, wondering how people will react, but honestly, it wouldn't bother me."

He reached down and touched her cheek. She was so soft.

Graceful. Whole. "It's not pretty, Kami. I don't want you to see what's left of me."

She furrowed her brow. "Aren't we two peas in a pod? I was so worried about what you'd think of me, I let you drift out of my life when you were probably the only steady thing I had. Now you're worried about what I'll think of your leg." Her hands tightened on him. "It's fine if you want to leave it on, but I wanted you to know you had options."

He blew out a breath. She made it all seem so logical. But could he do it? He'd never let anyone see his stump except his parents and medical personnel. "I just think it might be too much."

She raised her eyebrows and tilted her head. "For me . . . or you?"

He slid his open palm along her jaw, wanting her to understand, wishing he could tell her what he was really afraid of. He ground his teeth together. *Just say it.*

"Kami, I'm not the man you remember."

She didn't break his gaze. "No, you're so much more."

Did she mean that? "Do you hear what I'm saying?" he asked, wanting to be sure.

"Yes."

She closed her eyes, and his thumb traced her chin. *So silky.* He wanted to kiss her, but is that what she wanted? "Kami."

She let her hands trail up his chest. "Do what you need to do."

Was she still talking about his prosthetic? His stomach tightened at the thought of it, but his leg was ready to breathe for a while. "Okay."

He pulled his leg forward, bent at the knee, but she didn't move and blocked him from turning away. "Can I help?" she asked.

"If you're sure." She gave him "*the look*" again. He shrugged and pulled up his sweatpant leg. "Just press that release button there on the side." She did as he asked and the ratchet strap released. The artificial limb loosened, and she gently pulled on it until it was off.

"Is that it?"

"Not quite. I still have my liner on." He bent around her and carefully took off the stump sock until there was just his blue liner. "Are you really sure about this?" His heart was pounding through his chest. What if she turned away in disgust?

"Stop asking me that." Her bossy tone was back.

His chest squeezed as he thought of how wrong this could go, but he took off the liner with the ratchet strap attached. He let out a sigh of relief as soon as it was off. It felt good to let his skin breathe a bit. He hardly dared look to see Kami's reaction.

Kami's hand hovered over his stump, but she didn't touch it. "Does it hurt?"

"Sometimes I get phantom pains at night, but no, it healed

well." He looked down at his residual limb. It really was a nice-looking stump as far as stumps went.

"Go ahead and touch it if you want."

She was hesitant at first, but then ran her hand over what was left of his shin. The embarrassment he thought he'd feel never materialized. Instead, her cold hands running over his leg were sending shivers through his body that had nothing to do with the temperature in the room. "Is the prosthetic not fitted properly? Is that why it's bothering you?"

"No, it's not that." He thought for a moment about how he could explain it to her. "I imagine it's like when women have to wear high heels all day. It just feels good to take them off."

She nodded. "That makes sense." Lying back down against him, she was quiet for a moment. "It must have been so hard to get used to."

"It was." He wrapped an arm around her, amazed at how comfortable he felt discussing this with her. "I hated having to relearn how to walk and try to make it look natural. I had great doctors and therapists, though."

"I was thinking that earlier. You hardly even have a limp."

Her praise warmed him. "I've worked hard for that." In that one statement, all the months of sweat and pain were worth it. He let his hands wander through her hair. "Thanks."

"For what?" Her voice was soft and low.

"For tonight. For making me laugh. For making me feel normal again."

"You're welcome."

And he knew she meant it.

Chapter Six

She'd never had someone run their hands through her hair like this before, and it was wreaking havoc with her senses. It was mesmerizing and tender and yet everywhere he touched ignited a pull of attraction that had her spellbound. She may have helped him feel normal again, but she knew she'd never be normal again after this experience. She wanted more. "Is it your turn or my turn?"

"It's my turn. I took my prosthetic off for you, remember?"

She remembered. It was an experience she'd never forget. "And you haven't fidgeted once since you took it off. I can tell you're so much more comfortable."

"Definitely." His hands kept up their slow torture as they started down her hair, from her scalp to her shoulders. "I want to ask you your permission to do something, but I don't want it to be a dare. I want it to be your choice, not a challenge."

Her pulse pounded when his hands stopped at her neck, cupping her head. "Ask me what?"

He gently tipped her chin until she looked at him. "I want to kiss you."

The butterflies that had been mildly fluttering in her stomach were suddenly airborne and swooping in so hard she could hardly catch a breath. "What did you say?"

Jonah leaned down until he was a hair's breadth away from her mouth. "I need to kiss you."

He hesitated, and their eyes met. The kiss she'd dreamed about all through high school was about to happen, and it seemed right that they both paused to acknowledge that it could change everything. Looking into his eyes, all her girlish infatuations of the teen he'd once been mixed with the courageous man in front of her. She wanted his kiss and knew that whatever happened later, she wouldn't regret this moment.

Kami let her hands trail up his chest, looping them around his neck to pull him the last few millimeters to her. Their lips met, tentatively at first, but Kami pushed her hands through his hair, wanting more. He quickly caught up and matched her intensity until a very wet nose came between them.

"Magnus," Jonah ground out.

Kami couldn't help but laugh. "Well, you were worried about being left out in the cold earlier."

"He has terrible timing." But he was smiling and petting the dog. Lola came over to see what all the commotion was about.

"I've been accused of that myself a time or two." She pulled back and allowed the dogs into their small circle.

He resumed stroking her hair, the energy was still thrumming between them. "I've wanted to kiss you for so long."

What? She turned to him, her eyes wide. "No way. You were always telling me what a great friend I was and treated me like your best buddy. When did you want to kiss me?"

"Since the beginning of senior year." He smiled as her mouth dropped open in surprise.

How many times had she wished he saw her as girlfriend material? Her hand flew up in the air. "Why didn't you say something? I had a crush on you that whole time, but didn't want to ruin our friendship."

"I didn't want to lose you as a friend, either." His voice was low. "Every time I hugged you I imagined just going for it and kissing you. But you always seemed like you were happy with how things were, and I didn't want to change that. I told myself that being your star-gazing partner or just hanging out with you after the track meets was enough."

"We are idiots. That's exactly what I was thinking about you. Do you remember New Year's?" she bit her lip and looked down. "I thought for sure you'd kiss me then, even if we were just friends, because that's what everyone would be doing at midnight."

"But I kissed your forehead." He took her hand in his and tilted his head until she met his gaze. "I'm sorry."

"Well, it was probably for the best. We both had a lot of challenges headed our way." She squeezed his fingers. "But I never forgot you."

"I never forgot you, either. When my physical therapy was the hardest, I heard your voice in my head, telling me to get over myself and get it done." His voice was husky, as if he were reliving that time in his life. "I should never have let you go. Tried harder to keep in touch."

"Well, we have time to catch up now. If you're up for it," she murmured.

"Is that a challenge?" He leaned forward and gave her a quick kiss on the lips. "Because I'm definitely up for it."

Kami laughed as both dogs muscled their way in to give their own kisses. Jonah had to scoot back to make room for them. "Hey, Mag, I'm starting to see a pattern here," he said, giving his most disapproving look to Magnus.

"Me, too." She laughed and patted Lola's head. "Did you guys need some attention?"

Lola took the patting as a signal to climb on Kami's lap. "Oof, you're a little big for a lap dog." Magnus watched Lola on Kami's lap, as if he was waiting to see if she'd stay there or not.

Jonah leaned in close. "Look, Magnus can't decide whether to join Lola on your lap."

His breath tickled her ear, making her heart skip a beat. "Like a dog pile, you mean?"

Magnus twitched his ears as if he knew they were talking about him. Jonah chuckled. "He's a little more sedate in his attention seeking."

"Like his owner?"

Jonah bent to kiss the spot where her shoulder met her neck. "I'm happy to take any attention you give me. Or give you some attention of your own."

She tilted her head to give him better access and closed her eyes. "You do seem rather good at that." She licked her lips, her throat suddenly dry at his ministrations. "I am so glad Lola came over tonight."

"Me, too."

He trailed kisses up her neck to her ear, and she thought her heart might pound out of her chest. It was as if they'd picked up where they'd left off six years ago, only better. Her heart was racing as if she were running a sprint. Could they really start something after all these years?

Here in the dark with Jonah and the dogs, it seemed as if her life was finally coming together. All she needed was Ben and Hailey to make it perfect. For the first time since the accident, she was feeling optimistic about the entire situation, and thinking about Ben didn't send a wave of worry over her. She'd face whatever came in his recovery and she'd have Jonah in her corner to help. It was a heady feeling.

"Jonah, I—"

But her words were drowned out with the lights coming back on and the front door opening simultaneously. "He's probably asleep," Dr. Harrison said from the front hallway.

"I doubt he'd sleep through this storm," his wife retorted.

Kami froze. What would his parents think? Jonah's arms tightened around her middle. "Don't panic." But even with his comforting words, she braced for the look on his parents' faces when they saw them.

His mom and dad walked into the family room and his mom's expression was just as Kami expected. Her eyes wide, her mouth a perfect *O*.

"Hello, Kami," she finally said, obviously needing a moment to find her voice. "I didn't know Jonah was expecting company tonight."

"I wasn't," Jonah said as he reached for his liner and prosthetic.

Kami stood and grabbed the blanket, hoping she didn't have a guilty look on her face. "My dog got out and ended up over here," she explained while she folded it. "The storm was pretty bad, so

Jonah invited me to wait with him until it broke."

While she'd been talking to his parents, Jonah had finished attaching his prosthetic and stood up next to her. "How was the party?" he asked his dad.

How could he act so casual when she could hardly stop over-explaining?

"It was fun. Your mother was worried about you, so we braved the roads. Looks like everything was under control." His father's eyes dipped to the fireplace, where their mugs still sat.

"We'd just eaten dinner when the lights went out, and we had hot chocolate by the fire." She looked down at herself in Jonah's over-sized sweats. "And since my jeans were so wet, Jonah lent me some dry clothes." Kami didn't know why she was babbling. They hadn't done anything wrong, but it was his *parents*. And she'd known them practically her entire life.

"I'm just glad you were here." Jonah's mom put her purse down on the kitchen counter and turned to smile at them. A genuine, happy smile. In that moment, the awkwardness disappeared, and Kami relaxed. It was okay.

"How're Hailey and Ben? I just heard about the accident tonight," Mrs. Harrison said, sympathy lacing her tone.

"The doctors are watching them really close, but it looks like they'll be okay." Her voice hadn't trembled once when she spoke of them, and she was proud of herself.

"If you're up to it, I'd love for you to stay a little longer. You can tell me how I can help," Mrs. Harrison said. "And we don't want you to feel like you have to rush off."

"I really can't stay. I have an early start tomorrow, and Lola and I should be going." She felt Jonah's hand tighten on her arm.

He looked between Kami and his mom. "Well, maybe we can all meet at the movie festival tomorrow night? But only if you feel okay about leaving Ben and your sister for a while," Jonah said, meeting her eyes. "I know I could use a little more Christmas spirit, if you're up for it."

She nodded and didn't miss the surprised look that passed between Jonah's parents. This was a big deal for him, and he was including her. She focused on Jonah and smiled up at him, hoping he could see how much it meant to her that he wanted the closeness they'd shared tonight to continue as much as she did. How had she ever doubted that?

He slid his arm around her shoulder and gave it a squeeze. "Just let me get my coat and boots."

"Okay." She watched him head toward his room. Did he have a special prosthetic for his boots? She gathered up her jeans, then started toward the hall. "It was good to see you, Dr. and Mrs. Harrison."

"Nice to see you, too," his mother said, as she came around the kitchen island to hug her. "Thanks for keeping him company. I hope we see you a lot more around here."

"Me, too," Kami said, returning the hug. She called for Lola, who reluctantly came to her side. "You can visit Magnus another day, girl," she chided her dog.

"You both can," Jonah called from the living room. She walked in with both dogs on her heels to see him trying to jam his prosthetic into a boot. "I'll just be a minute." He expertly braced his arm against it and got his artificial foot to slide in. "Let me get your coat."

He grabbed it off the closet doorknob and helped her put it on. He took her hand, but before he opened the door, he stopped. "Oh, look."

Kami raised her face to see the mistletoe now hanging above the door. "Was that there all the time?" she asked with a laugh.

"Our little truth or dare game is over, so I don't have to tell." He touched her cheek and gave her a gentle kiss that was just long enough to make her knees turn to water.

"Merry Christmas," she said as they drew apart.

"Now it is." He tucked a piece of her hair behind her ear and Lola jumped up, pressing herself between them. Magnus must have thought it looked like fun so he joined in with a yip and a dance around their legs.

"Do you think the dogs planned this all along?" Kami's lips turned up in an exasperated grin as she tried to stay upright. She was glad Jonah was strong enough to hold them both up or the dogs would have definitely bowled them over.

"Lola does seem to know what she wants." His hands were sliding down her arms, and a shiver rippled through her.

Kami glanced down at the dogs before she pulled him close. "Just like her owner."

He laughed and kissed her as if he didn't want to let her go. Kami nearly pinched herself to see if she was dreaming. The last few days had been the most stressful of her life, and, in the space of one evening, her burden was so much lighter. More than that, her best friend was back and he'd wanted to kiss her for as long as she'd wanted to kiss him.

She'd never have predicted any of her girlish wishes would ever come true, but here she was, living the best one of all.

Kami could hardly wait for tomorrow.

Chapter Seven

The sun was just setting as Jonah and his parents pulled up to Kami's home to pick her up for the festival. Seeing her again was all he'd thought about since last night, but now the moment was here, he was nervous. He glanced down the block, noting she hadn't moved far from where her family had lived when she was in high school. The neighborhood had always been older, but was more on the side of shabby now.

Jonah got out and looked down at the snowy patches on the edges of the sidewalk that led to a porch with three steps. He groaned inwardly. Maneuvering ice and uneven ground with a prosthetic was daunting on his best day, but downright frightening when he wanted to impress Kami by being confident and coordinated.

He wiped his palms on the front of his jeans and then slowly walked up the sidewalk. Every snowy shadow taunted him with the possibility of being icy, but knowing his mother was watching from the car, he kept a steady pace. Climbing Kami's porch steps, he stopped for a second and took a breath, feeling a little rush of victory. He'd made it and hadn't fallen.

He knocked on the door and stepped back, smiling, as he heard Lola's bark announcing they had a visitor. Kami's house was small and had definitely seen better days, but there were Christmas lights framing the front window where he could see a small decorated tree in the living room. Whatever the house might lack in the newness department, Kami and her sister obviously made up for it with a homey feel.

Kami opened the door and gave him a grin. Just seeing the happiness in her eyes lifted his heart.

"Ready for a movie guaranteed to put you in the holiday spirit?" he asked.

"Definitely." Kami already had her coat on, but grabbed a scarf. She walked over to an open doorway barred by a child gate and gave Lola one last pat. "Be a good girl, I won't be too long."

Lola stared up at Kami with adoring eyes and when she walked away, the dog barked once, then sat down with a little whine.

"I'll bring her back to you safe and sound, girl," Jonah called out, as Kami locked the door behind her.

She started down the porch stairs and Jonah followed. He had to hold onto the railing, but let it go the moment he cleared the bottom step.

"I didn't want to take a chance of her escaping again, so I'm keeping her in the house while we're gone," Kami explained, turning her head so he could hear her. With only a narrow part of the sidewalk shoveled, they couldn't walk side by side.

"Magnus will be disappointed." Jonah was glad she was in front since he needed to concentrate on his steps and try to find a natural rhythm. He didn't want to force her to slow down because of him.

"I'm sorry the sidewalk isn't better shoveled. I hired one of the neighbor kids to do it and he tries his best," she said apologetically as she turned and faced him.

"It's good practice for me," he said, pulling his gaze away from the sidewalk and meeting her eyes. There wasn't any pity in them, just sincerity with a hint of shyness. Was she nervous about today, too?

She pulled her scarf tighter around her and changed the subject. "I heard they're playing *Miracle on 34th Street* tonight."

"I always liked that one." He waited for her to start walking again, but she moved to the very edge of the sidewalk instead, making room for them to walk together. It was a tight fit, though, and their hands nearly brushed each other with each step. He was tempted to just curl his fingers around hers. He wanted to touch her and remind himself that he wasn't dreaming, that they really had reconnected last night, but what if she had changed her mind about him? Things could look different in the light of day. And even if she hadn't changed her mind, what if he fell and took her down with him?

Deciding he was overthinking things, he threw caution to the wind and reached out for her. Kami slipped her hand into his as if she'd been waiting for his cue, and the warmth of her palm seeped into him, chasing away all his doubts. They'd found each other again and it was everything he'd ever imagined. Now he needed to stop worrying and enjoy the moment.

They walked toward the car where his parents were waiting. "I hope you don't mind my parents coming along. I think they were so excited I'd agreed to go out, they wanted to be there to witness it," he said ruefully.

Kami laughed as Jonah's mom waved to her from the passenger seat. "Have you really been that bad?"

Jonah nodded. "Yeah. I think this is the first time I've left the house since I got home. It's just . . . well, it's hard to be stared at and whispered about."

She slowed and he matched her steps. "You have to remember how much you mean to everyone in Hill Spring. You've been the golden boy since high school and now you're a returning war hero. People just want you to know they care."

Jonah immediately shook his head, wanting to dispel that myth. "I'm not a hero. I was just doing my job."

Kami gave him a penetrating gaze that brooked no argument. "You saved a man's life that day. Don't forget that."

They'd reached the car, but Jonah wished he had one more minute to ask her how she knew what had happened. Not many people did. But they couldn't stand outside talking while his parents were in the car waiting.

Filing his questions away for later, he opened the car door for Kami, then went around and got in on the other side. Hill Spring's town center wasn't far away, but he still enjoyed the drive. It was nice to be out of the house. Jonah hadn't realized until today how much of a hermit he'd become since he'd returned home.

"How's Ben?" Jonah asked. "When you texted earlier, you said there was some good news."

"He's responding to treatment and the doctor is really hopeful that he'll be able to recover completely." Kami couldn't keep the happiness out of her voice. "If things go well, I might be able to bring both him and Hailey home a few days after Christmas."

"That's wonderful," Jonah's mom said, turning so she could see Kami better. "You must be so relieved."

"I am. It's been a tough few days of wondering and waiting." Kami put her hand on the seat near Jonah's leg. He took the opportunity to intertwine his fingers with hers, feeling that little zing of awareness the moment he touched her.

"So have you suspended winter training until after the new year so you can concentrate on your family?" his dad asked, looking at them in the rearview mirror.

Kami settled back in her seat, her shoulder touching Jonah's. "I had the team doing some strength and circuit training while I was at the hospital. But we're having one more full practice run before Christmas break so I can chart their progress and give them a few things to work on when we pick it back up in January."

"Do you still run on the high school track?" Jonah asked. "That's got to be cold this time of year."

"Actually, the school got an indoor track a few years back and that has really helped our training. You should come see it sometime. I'd love to show you around," Kami said, tilting her head toward him and raising her eyebrows expectantly.

He nodded and she smiled before leaning forward toward his mom. "It's hard to believe Christmas break is right around the corner. Jonah told me you made some of your famous sugar cookies."

His mom laughed. "I should have invited you over to decorate with us, then Jonah wouldn't have been able to say no. Remember back in high school, when you two would compete for who had the best decorated sugar cookie? It was like you'd taken the competition off the track and brought it home." Her tone turned nostalgic. "It was so fun to watch you guys run."

Jonah shifted in his seat and was pleasantly surprised that the topic of his racing days didn't sting as much as it did just yesterday. Having Kami back had worked wonders on his attitude already. "I don't think there was even a question of who won best decorated cookie back then. That would be me."

"Well, I'd say you won for the cookie with the most icing," his mom said with a twinkle in her eye. "I think you used a pound of frosting on three cookies."

"That's what I said to him," Kami put in, trying to hold back a snort of laughter. "It's all about the frosting for him, not decorating."

"Having frosting on it means it *is* decorated," Jonah protested. "Who needs any candies or sprinkles? Besides, no one ever complained until today."

They all laughed and Jonah basked in the warm and light atmosphere. Everything was finally clicking into place, as if he was back to his old self. And none of it would have happened without Kami. She was the missing piece he'd been searching for all along. He looked down at their entwined fingers, noticing how she was a perfect fit, as if they had been made to hold each other. He lightly squeezed her hand, taking a mental snapshot of everything he was feeling so he could remember this moment forever.

All too soon, they'd found a great parking spot and were

headed into the theater. Jonah kept watching the faces of those around him, waiting for the whispers and stares. A few people watched him as they passed, but no one openly stared or pointed. He relaxed as they reached the lobby doors and his dad held it open for all of them. Maybe his leg was old news now and he wouldn't have to worry about being the town's main topic of conversation anymore.

As the doors closed behind them, they moved into the warmth of the theater and unzipped their coats. A group of carolers dressed up in old-fashioned clothing were singing in the far corner, looking like they'd stepped off a Christmas card. The concession stand was serving hot chocolate and Santa cookies. Each person in line looked happy and full of holiday cheer, the same as they had every year since Jonah and his parents had moved here. It was so familiar and with a pang, Jonah realized how much he'd missed all this. The shades of his childhood were all wrapped up in the traditions of the season and the people at his side.

His parents walked a few steps in front as they went to buy their tickets to the show. Jonah and Kami were trying to keep up, but the crowd pressed in on them and soon they couldn't see his parents anymore. Jonah kept a firm grip on Kami's hand as people darted in front and jostled them from behind. What if he lost his balance? "Kam, can we move to the side? I don't want to embarrass you by falling on my face."

"Don't worry, I've got a plan," she said, surprising him with a grin. "If you fall, I'll just turn to the person next to me and say, hey, why'd you push him?"

"Or you could just keep walking and pretend you don't know me." He was only half-joking, wanting to see her reaction.

She kept a smile on her face and shook her head. "I wouldn't leave a date to be trampled. Nope, you're stuck with me."

Relief rushed over him at her words, but he was still going to do all he could to stay upright. She moved closer as if she instinctively knew he needed extra support and he was grateful. They'd just established a good pace when a familiar face broke from the crowd and approached them. He was dressed in immaculately pressed tan slacks with a light blue button-down shirt. Though he looked older, Jonah was immediately transported back to high school. How many times had he competed in the 400 meter race against Tim Cross?

Tim ignored Jonah and zeroed in on Kami. He gave her a quick once-over, her red flannel shirt and curve-hugging jeans bringing an appreciative smile to his face. Jonah repressed a frown.

"Hey, I'm surprised to see you here," Tim said, still acting like he hadn't noticed Jonah. "How's Ben?"

"He's good. I might be able to bring him home soon." Kami turned to the left and tilted her head toward him. "Tim, you remember Jonah?" Her hand tightened around Jonah's and he moved closer.

Tim finally acknowledged him with a smile that was as fake as Jonah's prosthetic foot. "Of course. Sorry to hear about your leg."

"Thanks." Jonah groaned inwardly, hoping the conversation wouldn't turn to questions about his amputation. He quickly glanced behind Tim, trying to spot his parents so they'd have an excuse to leave if he needed one, but didn't see them. "It's been a long time."

"Yeah, I think the last time we saw each other was at the high school track and field championship. You took first, but I attribute it to your running partner." He turned on the charm for Kami, trying to dazzle her with a wide grin, but Jonah caught his uneasy glance at their clasped hands. "Which is why I'm glad I snagged her for my own running partner. We're still signing up for that 10K, right Kam?"

Jonah drew his eyebrows down. Back in high school, he was the only one Kami had allowed to shorten her name. What did Tim mean to her? A tiny sliver of jealousy poked into his heart, but when she moved closer to Jonah so another couple could get around them, the feeling eased. Whatever had happened in the past, she was with him now.

"Yeah, I've nearly got everything ready. Quite a few from the track team are signing up, too," she told him, biting her lip. "I hope it's a good experience for them."

"Well, if you're up for another practice run sometime this week, I'm happy to take you." He squeezed in on Kami's other side and held her elbow. "I thought we had a lot of fun last time."

Kami shifted away, looking uncomfortable. "I think we all had a good run."

"I don't imagine you get much running in these days," Tim said, giving Jonah's prosthetic foot a pointed look, before lifting his eyes to his face.

Jonah could hardly take his eyes off Tim's hand that still rested on Kami's elbow. The old rivalry was starting to rise in him. "Actually, I had some really good physical therapy and, with my running blade, I was nearly back to my high school times." He gently touched Kami's back and stepped forward, breaking Tim's hold on her. "Sorry, Tim, but we don't want to miss the movie. Maybe we can catch up another time."

Tim didn't move and the crowd was hemming them in so Jonah couldn't easily get around him. He met Tim's gaze and all Jonah saw there was cold resentment. He obviously still had more to say and Jonah braced himself for it.

But Tim ignored Jonah completely and inched closer to Kami. "He's only been home for a week and you're already groveling at his feet for any crumbs of attention, just like you did in high school. Don't you have any self-respect?"

Jonah stiffened and recoiled, pulling Kami close, as if he could ward off the effect of his words. "That's enough. We're leaving,"

Jonah tried to move away, but Kami stood rooted in place, glaring at Tim. Every muscle in her body had tensed and contained fury rolled off of her in waves. Jonah had so rarely seen her angry, he was momentarily stunned.

Her free hand clenched into a fist as she looked up at Tim. "It's always been about beating Jonah, hasn't it? You didn't want to be my friend, you were trying to take Jonah's place in my life."

Tim didn't back down. "Take a good look at what's going on here, Kami. He kept you at arms' length in high school. He dropped you like an old pair of track shoes when he left town. You haven't heard from him in years, and now he's back and you're sucked in again. Is it out of pity? Because I could understand that. I mean, the guy lost a foot and needs sympathy, but he doesn't deserve you. He never did."

Kami gave him an icy stare and moved closer until she was nearly nose to nose with Tim. "You don't know what you're talking about. You've always been jealous of Jonah and now you're taking cheap shots at him." She was brusque, as if she was wasting her time and couldn't wait to get away. "And what I feel for Jonah is none of your business. It never has been."

Tim shook his head as he looked between them. "Whatever. Maybe you two do deserve each other. But if you ever get tired of sitting around with him and want to go running or need help training the kids, give me a call." He gave them both a sullen glance before he turned and moved away.

"Don't hold your breath," Kami said loudly, so he could hear over the crowd. She rolled her shoulders, but still looked like she wanted to punch something.

Jonah watched him go, rubbing his hand over her upper arm hoping to calm her and himself. "Are you okay?"

"Yeah." She sucked in some air and let it out slowly as if she'd just finished a sprint and was walking it off.

"He's still the same jerk I remember from high school." Jonah hadn't thought about Tim in years, but he'd obviously been thinking about Jonah. Some of his comments had struck a nerve, though. To an outsider, it could have appeared as if Jonah had dropped her after high school. He wished he could go back and change that, but at least, he'd discussed it with Kami last night and they both understood what happened.

"I actually thought he'd changed," Kami said, relaxing into his embrace. "He was really nice to me and offered to help get the team ready for the 10K. I forgot how jealous he was of you."

He kissed her temple, the flowery smell of her shampoo drifting to his nose. It was a different scent from when he'd known her before, but he liked it. "Thanks for standing up for me. I was scared for him when I saw the look on your face."

She glanced up at Jonah, the anger still lingering in the

tightness around her lips and eyes. "Do you think I got my point across?"

"Let's just say I've decided never to make you mad, if I can help it." Jonah squeezed her shoulder and looked scared. She laughed as he'd hoped she would.

The crowd had thinned a bit and they walked toward his parents who were waiting for them near the theater entrance. The mood was nearly back to how it had been before meeting up with Tim—just happy to be together. The carolers had finished their last song and were packing up while everyone was going in to take their seats.

They walked into the theater and Kami leaned in and whispered, "Were you telling the truth? Were you hitting your old high school times with your running blade?"

"Well, I hit it, once," Jonah admitted sheepishly. "It was a work in progress before I stopped."

"Would you like to do a run with me?" she asked as they took their seats.

A part of him shouted no, that if he fell, he'd be embarrassed. But the pull of running beside Kami again shot a little adrenaline through his system. "I'd love to."

"Are you sure?" She held his gaze and even in a theater full of people, for just a moment, it was as if they were alone and she could read all his thoughts and emotions.

He nodded and the corners of her mouth quirked up in a slow smile. He wished they were truly alone so he could kiss her. For the moment, all he could do was caress the soft skin of her hand with his thumb, but as the lights went down, he was making plans that ended with him and Kami all by themselves.

Chapter Eight

Miracle on 34th Street was one of Kami's favorite movies, but she'd never cried during it before. Now she was sitting in a darkened theater trying to discreetly wipe away her tears before the lights came up. Her emotions had been so close to the surface lately that she couldn't hold them back during the movie. Christmas really did feel like a time of miracles and she'd had a few of her own lately. Her sister and Ben were going to be fine. And Jonah was back in her life. She never would have imagined finding him again or finally admitting their feelings for each other, even if she'd sat on Santa's lap and wished for it every year. She couldn't explain how or why it had happened, but she was grateful it had.

In addition to trying to keep her emotions in check, she'd also had a hard time concentrating with Jonah right next to her. He was so familiar, yet at the same time, he was different. There were shadows in his eyes and sometimes his smile seemed forced. But their shared memories and foundation of friendship created an intimacy between them that had allowed them to pick up where they left off and move forward as if no time had passed. She'd never felt so connected to anyone else and though things were moving fast, it was right. She knew it. Even holding his hand gave her a sense of coming home.

When the credits finally ended, she stood, and Jonah reached out to help her put on her coat. "Do you mind if we slip over and take a picture of the decorations on the city tree? I promised Ben I would. This is the first year we've missed the tree lighting ceremony."

Jonah looked surprised, but quickly nodded. "Sure. Is he big on Christmas decorations or something? I'm surprised a kid his age would care about that."

"For the last couple of years the city has had children make a laminated snowflake with their Christmas wishes on it and they use them to decorate the tree. Ben is sure that's how Santa remembers what he's asked for. I got it to the decorating committee and he just wants proof that it was hung on the tree." Kami wadded up her scarf and put it in her pocket. "Of course all he's asked for is a Captain America doll."

"Do boys call it a doll?" Jonah teased. "Action figure sounds more manly."

She threw up her hands in mock exasperation. "Whatever it's

called, that's what he wants." She moved to the aisle behind his mother. "I haven't had a chance to finish my Christmas shopping, so I really need to move that up on my to do list before they're all sold out of Captain America stuff."

"Maybe I could go shopping with you and pick something out for my parents." He gave her a tentative smile and her heart melted a bit. He'd softened and let down his defenses since she'd first seen him. Kami was enjoying the glimpses of the easygoing person he'd once been and getting to know the more cautious man he'd become.

As they walked into the lobby, Jonah's mom turned to Kami. "I heard you say you were going to the city park to take a picture of the tree. Do you want to meet us at the diner for dessert afterward?" she asked. "We were going to get some of Betsy's homemade apple pie."

"That's a great idea," Kami said. "No one should ever resist a craving for homemade apple pie."

"We'll see you in a little while then," his mom said, giving Jonah a bright smile. "Thanks for coming with us, sweetheart. It was fun to be together as a family again."

Jonah agreed and Kami was surprised at how natural it felt to be included in that statement. Jonah put his hand at her back and guided her out of the theater and down the street, dodging the crowds and staying on the edges as they headed toward the city park. There were so many Christmas lights decorating the streetlamps up and down Main Street. Combined with the festive spirit of the shoppers bustling around them, the night seemed magical. Kami leaned closer to Jonah and he put his arm around her. They'd both been quiet since they left the theater and she wondered what he was thinking about.

"Penny for your thoughts," he said, pulling her against him.

She laughed and tilted her chin to look up at him. "I was just wondering what you were thinking! Isn't it crazy that two days ago I couldn't have imagined having you back in my life."

His expression turned serious, the muscle in his jaw working. She waited patiently, knowing that whatever he was going to say was important to him.

He swallowed before he spoke. "Kami, I thought about you a lot while I was gone, you know, and wondered what you were doing. You weren't tossed away like old track shoes. When you showed up yesterday, it felt like we'd never been apart and I knew I'd made a big mistake when I didn't try harder to keep in touch."

Any doubts she'd had about him disappeared and warmth settled over her, his words like a comforting quilt.

"I know you did and I thought about you, too. But don't let Tim get inside your head. He doesn't have any clue what's between us." She pressed her side against him, feeling his strength even as he worked to keep his steps steady and even.

"I won't even mention his name again." He bent and quickly kissed her on the lips. "But one thing is for sure. Lola must have known how much Magnus and I needed you."

Had that really only happened yesterday? She touched his cheek. "Or maybe it's the other way around and she knew *I* needed *you.*"

Jonah stopped walking and stood there for a moment, looking at her. His eyes seemed to see down to her soul and she gazed back, letting him in. He took her hand and pulled her off the sidewalk until they were under a tree on the edge of the city park. He cupped her head and let his thumb stroke her cheek.

"Do you know how amazing you are?" he whispered before he kissed her.

Kami reveled in the sensations he evoked in her, the butterflies swooping and soaring through her middle. Heat rushed through her veins and she stretched her arms around his neck, running her hands through his hair. He groaned and deepened the kiss, taking a half step back to anchor them better. Kami was completely lost in the moment when she felt him pull away, falling into the snow and pulling her down on top of him.

It took a few seconds before her brain could catch up from the blazing intensity of his kiss to suddenly being thrust into a snow bank.

"Are you okay?" she asked, looking down at him. He had his

hands over his eyes and his lips were pressed tightly together. "Did you hurt yourself?"

"Maybe my pride," he finally said, his voice strained. "Are you hurt?"

"I'm fine." She heard a small groan escape from him, which he quickly stifled. Was he in pain and didn't want to tell her? She peeled his hand away from his face. "What's wrong?"

He puffed out a breath of frustration. "Kami, I can't even hold you long enough to kiss you properly without falling over." He looked at her, the shadows in his eyes hiding the light that had been there moments before.

"Jonah," she said carefully, knowing this was a sensitive topic for him. "You do realize that even people with two feet fall on ice and snow." She touched her thumb to his bottom lip and gave a dramatic sigh. "Maybe this is the universe telling us to cool it."

He was quiet for a beat, but then joined in her teasing. "After waiting six years, don't you think the universe could be a little more understanding?"

He gave her a small smile and she chuckled as she got off his chest so he could sit up. He put his hands on his knees and she sat beside him.

Looking over at her, he shook his head. "It really doesn't bother you that I have limitations? I'm not even close to the same guy I was when you knew me before."

"I'm not the same as I was, either. Nobody is," she said, nudging his shoulder, suddenly wanting him to know what she felt when she looked at him. "Do you know what I thought about when I heard you'd been in an explosion and had lost a foot?" He shook his head. "All I could think was how grateful I was that you were still alive. *You* were still in this world. That's what mattered. I don't care about your missing foot because *you* are here."

He closed his eyes and put his arm around her, pulling her close and kissing her hair. She could feel tears pricking the back of her throat.

"I've missed you," he whispered into her ear. "So much."

The moment was so profound, Kami didn't want to say anything to mar it. He grazed her cheek with his knuckles, tilting her chin upward, sealing the feelings they'd shared with a kiss. His lips moved over hers so tenderly at first, then fiercely, possessively. Her heart hammered in her chest. He was her other half. She'd always known it and now she was experiencing it. Her hand skimmed over his jaw and she was once again lost in him—in them.

Breathless, Jonah drew away, touching his forehead to hers. "We need to get you out of the cold. Your jeans are probably as soaked as they were yesterday."

She laughed. "Pretty close. I think I'm going to have to start carrying extra clothes with me whenever I'm around you."

With one last kiss, she stood and reached down to help him up. He hesitated, looking at her hand, but finally grabbed it and got to his feet with a little hop step. She brushed the snow off her backside, and he did the same, but once they were done, his arm came around her again, enfolding her in his warmth. She snuggled close, wrapping her arms around his waist. They could lean on each other, physically and emotionally, and it was a reassurance to her that he seemed to want it as much as she did.

They slowly strolled to the middle of the city park where a stately old pine tree stood decorated with colorful balls, lights, and the homemade snowflakes. Kami circled the tree until she found Ben's. It was halfway up and near the middle.

"He's going to love that. It'll be easy for Santa to spot." She took several pictures from all different angles and then Jonah took one of her pointing to the exact snowflake.

"Perfect." He handed her phone back. "And I don't just mean the tree," he said with a wink.

She rolled her eyes and shook her head, but a flush crept up her neck at the compliment. "I can't wait for Ben to see that they used the blue and purple lights this year. They're his favorite," Kami said, changing the subject as she scrolled through the pictures she'd gotten.

"I can't wait to meet him," Jonah told her. "He sounds like a great kid."

"Why don't you come with me tomorrow? Then, if you're up for it, I can show you the new track, maybe go for a little run together and test out your running blade?" Her voice was nonchalant, but every part of her was hoping he'd say yes to both of those things.

"That sounds great." He didn't hesitate at all this time and she was encouraged. The more she was with him, the more it seemed like he was relaxing about his injury.

"Can I ask you something?" She glanced up at him and waited until he nodded. "Why did you stop running during physical therapy?"

He thought for a moment. "It's hard to explain. Part of me felt like I was trying to go back to who I was, when I would never be him again. I was still struggling to accept what my injury meant, so I gave up on running so I could focus on a new me."

"So you didn't think the new you would be a runner?" She couldn't imagine Jonah not running, but at the same time, it was easy to understand how what had once brought so much joy could now bring pain after a loss like he'd suffered.

"I didn't know what the new me was going to be like. I've been trying to figure that out." He squeezed her shoulder. "But I'd like to run with you again and see how it feels."

She nodded, glad that the hope and light in his eyes were back. That's what mattered, nothing else.

They made it to the diner and found his parents in a back booth. Four pieces of apple pie were on the table, two of them smothered in ice cream. Kami's mouth watered just looking at them.

"You remembered," she said to Jonah's mom, a happy sigh escaping her.

"How could I forget?" his mother said, patting the seat next to her. "Even in the coldest part of winter, hot apple pie with ice cream was your favorite." Before Kami could sit down, his mom noticed how wet their jeans were. "Did something happen?"

"I fell," Jonah said calmly as he slid onto the vinyl seat. "In a snow bank."

His mom's grip on her fork tightened and her smile was frozen in place. "Are you all right?"

He nodded and glanced over at Kami with a mischievous look in his eye. "Yeah. Kami kept me warm until I could get back on my feet."

She could feel her cheeks heat at the innuendo in his tone. In front of his parents! "Maybe next time I'll push you in myself," she said, raising her eyebrows and giving him "the look."

They laughed and an air of closeness and warmth settled over their group. Kami got out her phone and showed them the pictures she'd taken of the tree. "I'm so excited to show Ben where his snowflake ended up. It's in the perfect spot." She put her phone back in her pocket. "I think we're going to hold off on opening presents until he's released from the hospital. It just won't be Christmas until Ben and Hailey are home."

Dee, the waitress at Betsy's Diner for as long as Kami could remember, came over and stopped next to the table. "Jonah, I'm surprised to see you out and about, but I'm glad you're here. How does it feel to be a returning war hero?"

She didn't notice that Jonah's smile had disappeared and his whole body had tensed at her words.

"I heard you saved your buddy that was standing close to you when the bomb went off. It's lucky neither of you were killed." Dee continued, with a hand on her ample hip. "Way to do us proud, though."

Jonah's jaw was clenched, but he gave her a crisp nod, without saying anything. Kami jumped in. "Dee, can I get a hot chocolate? That would be perfect with my pie,"

"Hot chocolate for everyone," Jonah's father added. He hadn't seemed to notice how uncomfortable his son was, either. How could Kami be the only one to see it?

Dee tapped her hand on the table. "I'll bring it right out. Don't be a stranger, Jonah. And come back in soon so we can catch up one of these days and you can tell me the rest of the story," she said, before she walked away.

Jonah let out a slow breath when she was gone. Kami took his hand under the table and squeezed it. "She only asks because she cares about you," Kami murmured.

Jonah closed his eyes for a moment, retreating into himself. "It's so awkward. And I hate reliving that day."

His parents looked between them, finally realizing something was wrong, but obviously unsure of what to say.

Kami moved closer to his side. "Once people have something else to talk about, you'll be old news." Resting her chin in her palm, she creased her brow in thought. "We just need something to take their minds off of you. Maybe we could start a rumor about a Bigfoot sighting in the city park."

"Or maybe we could start a poll at your dad's office about what constitutes a decorated cookie—is frosting enough or do you need candies and sprinkles?" His mom suggested, reaching over and putting her hand on Jonah's arm. "I could even bring samples."

"Samples at the office would be my vote," her dad said with a nod. "Definitely."

The tension in Jonah's eyes softened and he gave their suggestions a half-grin. It was enough for now. Kami sat back and took another bite of pie. Everyone in town was still getting used to the new normal of Jonah being home and the changes he'd made in his life. Even Jonah was trying to figure out where he fit. It was going to take some time, but eventually, acceptance for the man

Jonah was now would come, for him, as well as the people who had known him since he was a teen.

And, if he'd let her, she'd be there every step of the way.

Chapter Nine

Jonah rolled down the car window and let the cold, wintry air rush over him. He was profoundly grateful for the level of freedom he still had in being able to get behind the wheel and drive somewhere. If he'd lost his right foot, driving a car would have been a lot more complicated, but it turned out to be one of the few things he hadn't had to relearn after his injury. Although he hadn't driven much since he got out of the hospital, he was appreciating the simple pleasure of it today.

He pulled up to Kami's house and parked in front, briefly checking his appearance in the rearview mirror. His hair was starting to grow in from his military buzz cut and he was getting used to the look. It definitely took more care than the buzz did, though.

Walking to the front door was nearly a repeat of yesterday, only today, he wasn't nervous. Something had changed after he'd fallen in the city park last night. Her easy acceptance had sunk deep into his core—and it was a profound relief that he didn't have to hide any part of himself from her.

He knocked and once again heard Lola's barking. Kami opened the door and Lola was dancing around her legs. "Can you come in for a minute? I'm not quite ready."

"Sure," he said, as he stepped inside and gave her a quick kiss on the cheek. He barely held off Lola's jump onto his legs, reaching down just in time to give her a scratch behind the ears.

Kami watched them, a wide smile on her face. "Take a seat and I'll be right back," she said as she waved toward her living room.

"Sounds good." He unzipped his coat and, with an excited Lola at his side, he stepped carefully through the hall into the small living room.

Instead of sitting down, he wandered to her bookcases, looking at what was on her shelf. It was mostly kids books and fairy tales on the lower shelves, with all her Runners World magazines above them. Those were obviously the two things in the world that were her top priorities— Ben and running. A few pictures were scattered in between the stacks of books and magazines, mostly of Ben, but there were a couple of Lola and some of her and her sister. He drew a picture of Ben closer, noticing that he had the same light brown hair as Kami. If she ever had kids of her own, they'd probably look just like him.

"Okay, I think I've got everything," she said, coming into the room. Lola abandoned him to go to Kami's side "I won't have time to come back and change for practice, so I wanted to pack my duffel." She held it up. "Did you grab everything you'll need?"

"Yep," he said as he walked toward her and took her duffel. "Let me carry that for you."

"Thanks. Let me just get Lola settled and we can go." She smiled and pecked him on the cheek, lingering for an extra moment. He raised his eyebrows and she gave him a saucy grin. It would be very easy to get used to being kissed by her regularly and often.

Once the dog had been corralled, with promises of treats and an extra long run when Kami got back, it didn't take long before they were on the road to the hospital.

"I got Ben a little present," Jonah told her as they drove away. "I hope you don't mind."

"He loves presents. And he might need a distraction today. He's getting anxious to come home." She looked down at her hands. "I can't wait for him to be released. The house is way too quiet without him and Hailey there."

"What's your sister's prognosis? Will she be coming home soon?" he asked, as he stopped at a red light.

"She's doing a lot better." Kami let out a long breath. "It's been hard, though. For the past year, I've been trying to back off a little bit and let Hailey be more of a mother figure to Ben. But since the accident I've kind of fallen back into the role of mothering them both."

"I can imagine. Has being a mom been difficult for Hailey?" Jonah only remembered a rebellious teen. It was strange to think of Hailey as anyone's mother.

"She had a tough time at first, but in the last year she's really stepped up. I'm so proud of her. She's even taking classes at the community college." Kami adjusted her seat belt and turned so she was nearly facing him. "It's been harder than I thought to let her be more of a mom. I was the one who nursed Ben through colic, who took him to the doctor, read to him, and potty-trained him. Hailey was so young it was easy to take over. I loved doing it."

"She was lucky to have you," Jonah said quietly.

"But I'm not Ben's mom. I don't want to take anything away from Hailey, so I'm working hard to let her be the central figure in Ben's life." She twisted her hands in her lap. "I guess I'm afraid that he'll forget me."

Jonah took her hand and covered it with his own. "He won't. No matter what happens you'll always have a bond with him."

Kami's shoulders slumped as if they held the weight of the world on them. "I hope so."

Still keeping his eyes on the road, he pulled her hand to his mouth and kissed the back of her fingers. She was baring her deepest fears to him and he wanted to do more than hold her hand. "You're unforgettable, believe me."

She gave him a small smile as they pulled into the hospital parking lot. After finding a spot fairly close to the door, they walked inside. The hospital smell assaulted Jonah the moment he stepped into the building. It was so familiar and had been a smell that had clung to him even after he came home. It reminded him of his injury, the things he'd suffered, but also that he'd been able to leave. He was home and rebuilding his life. That felt good.

They went through security to the pediatric ward and Kami greeted several of the nurses. "He's doing great today," one of them said to her. "He'll be happy to see you."

Kami's earlier pensiveness was gone and she was nearly humming with happiness as they walked into Ben's room. "How's my Benny Bear?" she called out as she opened the door.

"Aunt Kam," the little boy said, turning his blonde head toward her with a grin. "I missed you."

He looked small in the bed, the bandage on his forehead making him look even more fragile, as if breathing too hard could hurt him. But Kami didn't even blink an eye and went right to him, her arms outstretched.

She hugged him, careful of the tubes and monitors that were connected to him. "How are you feeling, sweetheart?"

"Good. I'm almost better I think." He held up two fingers. "Maybe I can come home in two days."

"Maybe," she said, as she sat down next to him on the bed. She glanced behind her. "I brought someone to meet you. My friend, Jonah."

"Hi," Ben said, giving him a shy smile.

Jonah moved forward to stand by Kami. "Hey, Ben. When your Aunt Kam told me you were in the hospital, I thought maybe you could use a little present to cheer you up." Jonah pulled the gift bag from behind his back.

Ben's eyes lit up. "Really?" Jonah gave it to him and Kami helped him unwrap it. "Cool! It's a Captain America." He hugged the figure to him. "I asked Santa to bring him to me, but now he doesn't have to."

Jonah smiled, glad he'd gone with the action figure instead of the Captain America blanket he'd seen. "I'm glad you like him. He's one of my favorite superheroes and now he can watch over you until it's time for you to come home from the hospital."

"Jonah used to be a soldier, just like Captain America, did you know that?" Kami ruffled his hair. "And he was very brave, too."

"Really?" Ben's eyes widened. "Have you ever saved somebody's life like Captain America? Or chased bad guys?"

Jonah shifted uncomfortably. He didn't really have any war stories appropriate for a little boy. "Well, I don't think there's anyone as good as Captain America, do you?"

Ben shook his head. "He's definitely the best."

"How do you even know about Captain America?" Jonah asked, moving to sit in the chair next to the bed. "Did you go to the movie?"

"No, my mom said I was too little. But Kaden at school saw it with his older brother and he told me all about it. We play Captain America vs. Iron Man at recess and I'm always Captain America." His looked at the action figure in his hand with reverence and Jonah couldn't hold back a smile.

"That's a good choice. When I was about your age, we would always play Batman and Superman at school." He glanced up at Kami still perched on the bed. "Well, until I met your Aunt Kam. Then she made me run with her all the time."

Ben nodded, as if he expected that, but his attention was focused on the Captain America doll. "Yeah, she likes running."

"We're going for a run today," Kami said, straightening Ben's blankets. "Jonah's out of practice, so I'm going to help him start again."

"Mom said she's coming to have lunch with me," Ben told them, as he fiddled with the shield on the Captain America doll. He grinned when he finally figured out how to detach it. "She's feeling lots better, too."

"And here I am," a voice said from the doorway. Hailey was

in a wheelchair, her face bruised and swollen. She rolled herself inside. "How's my Benny Bear?"

"My headache is going away," he told her proudly. "And Aunt Kam's friend Jonah brought me a Captain America!" He held up the doll.

"That's great." Hailey's eyes darted to Jonah and her mouth nearly dropped open in surprise, but to her credit, she recovered quickly. "It's been a long time, Jonah."

"It has." He shifted forward to stand, but Hailey held up her hand.

"You don't have to stand on my account." She rolled closer to the bed. "How have you been?"

"A little better than you, I think. How are *you* feeling?" Jonah was surprised that beyond the swelling on her face, it was hard to tell that she was injured. But he knew better than anyone that, more often than not, there were less obvious injuries to deal with, both physical and emotional.

"Like I was run over by a truck." She grimaced and put her hand on her side. "But the good news is I can go home when Ben does."

Kami looked at her sister and Jonah only saw genuine happiness in her face. When she turned her gaze to Ben, however, the underlying love with a thread of longing came through.

"I'll let you two get to your lunch then. Jonah's coming over to the track with me today, but I'll come back after dinner to say goodnight." She spoke quickly, as if she knew she had to get the words out before she changed her mind.

Hailey didn't seem to notice anything amiss with her sister. She leaned forward with a mischievous grin on her face. "And hopefully you'll have a few more things to tell me, too. It's been a while since we talked about your dating life."

Kami ducked her head and she blushed. "I don't know what you mean," she said as she bent and kissed Ben's forehead. "I'll see you guys later."

Hailey's laugh followed them as they left the room.

"What are you going to tell her?" Jonah asked as they walked by the nurses' station and headed for the elevators. "Because you know she isn't going to let it go."

And Hailey wasn't the only one interested to hear what Kami's thoughts were on Jonah and their renewed relationship.

"What *should* I tell her?" Kami countered, giving him a side eye and a smile.

They stopped in front of the elevators and he pushed the down button. Well, if she was going to wait for him to make the first move, he was up for the challenge.

"I guess you could say we were stranded in a snowstorm with two matchmaking dogs, so we just gave in and decided that it was meant to be." He took her hand, relishing the fact that he could.

"Short, sweet, and true."

Kami gave a low laugh as she lifted her eyes and met his gaze. The heat between them flared. "I don't know why I didn't think of that."

He leaned in and touched her hair. The sun coming through the window behind them gave her a halo effect, like an angel come to life in front of him. Her light drew him in, chasing away any shadows, but before he could claim a kiss, the elevator dinged and the doors whooshed open.

She gave him a rueful grin, as if she knew the direction of his thoughts. They both stepped aside to let the people off before they took their place inside.

He cleared his throat. "So, how long do we have until the track kids show up?" he asked, trying to take his mind off of stealing a kiss in the elevator.

"We'll have the track to ourselves for about an hour." She looked over at him. "You're not nervous are you?"

"Maybe a little. It's been a while and I want to impress you." The elevator doors opened and the old fears resurfaced at the same time. He held her gaze for a second longer. "Or at the very least, I don't want to fall."

"You impress me just by being you." She reached over and took his hand as they walked through the parking lot toward the car. "Remember your old warm-up routine when we were in high

104

school? Maybe you should try that again."

"How could I ever forget the 80s music and green gummy bears?" Jonah said as he climbed into the car. "Nothing takes your mind off of pre-race jitters better than trying to chew a gummy bear while you're rocking out to Hall and Oates. But I didn't bring either of those things with me."

"I've got a bag of gummy bears in my office, but I don't think I have any 80s music. The kids like all the modern songs with beats that will rock the equipment when we turn it up and put it on the speaker system."

"Yeah, my physical therapist liked that stuff for my sessions as well." He adjusted his prosthetic foot, glad they weren't running at night and that his stump wasn't tired or aching. Even with a great fit, after having a prosthetic on all day, by the time evening rolled around, he was always ready to take it off.

They pulled into the high school lot and parked. Kami grabbed her duffel from the back seat and got out of the car. "You ready?"

"As ready as I'll ever be." He pulled his own duffel out and looked over at the high school. His heart accelerated, almost exactly like it had before a race. Kami was right. His pre-race routine from years ago might be the calm that he needed. "And I'm going to take you up on those gummy bears. I hope you've got some green ones."

"We might have to dig for those." She took out some keys and unlocked the high school doors. "We've got so many memories here, don't we? The classes, the teachers, the races."

"Almost all good memories, too. Except for Mr. Peaslee. I could have done without his class." She laughed and he followed her into the main hall and looked around. The school smelled the same. The same pale green lockers lined each side. The hallways to the gym had the same mirrors with motivation posters above them. "It's almost like we never left."

They walked to the gym, but she bypassed those doors for a larger, newer one beyond it. "The new indoor track," she announced as she pushed it open.

He walked in and was impressed by the state of the art, six-lane track. "This is amazing," he said. "I bet you were thrilled to have a practice facility like this."

"I was. It's helped immensely with our training." She went over to a bench and set her duffel bag down to unzip it. "I'm going to go into the women's locker room and change. I'll be right back."

"Can you bring back the gummy bears?" he said, putting his own duffel next to hers.

"Sure," she smiled. "Should I try to find some Hall and Oates?"

"Nah, we'll change things up today. You can be my motivation. How's your singing?" He was trying to keep things light, but when he unzipped his bag and looked down at his running blade, his heart ratcheted up a notch. He was definitely going to need something to distract him. He hadn't used the blade in months. Squaring his shoulders, he took a breath. *It'll be okay.*

Kami watched him thoughtfully for a moment. "Jonah, we don't have to do this today."

He immediately shook his head. After psyching himself up for this, he wasn't going to back out now. "I'm good. Really."

She raised an eyebrow, but nodded before she turned to make her way across the track. "Okay, I'll be right back."

He picked up his bag and went to the other side, where a sign indicated the men's locker rooms were. He changed into running shorts and a shirt, looking down at his prosthetic. Sitting down, he took it off and put on a fresh liner and sock. Maneuvering his stump into the socket of the running blade, he rolled up the suction sleeve.

The running blade was a little longer than his normal foot because when he ran, he compressed the spring more than when he was just walking. It felt good, though, and he sucked in a breath. No matter what happened, it would be okay. He could do it. Standing, he stashed his normal prosthetic in his duffel and slung it over his shoulder.

Kami was already warming up when he got back to the track. She looked so much like the girl he'd known in high school with her ponytail, Hill Spring Warriors t-shirt and running shorts. She smiled and handed him a small bag of gummy bears when he got close enough. "Just like old times."

It really was. Jonah dug out a few green ones, hoping they were still lucky for him. Once they'd stretched, they started a slow jog around the track. So far, Jonah was feeling good and the running blade had just the right spring.

After two laps, he picked up the pace. "I don't want you to take it easy on me or stay back because of me," he warned. "If you need to go faster, go ahead."

She nodded, but stayed at his side. It wasn't long before all thoughts of his prosthetic and injury was pushed to the side as he settled into a rhythm and felt the rush of running roll through him. There weren't any words to describe having Kami running next to him, pushing his body to its limits with a track underneath him. Students were starting to file in, but they only became a part of the blur as he ran past. He wanted to throw his arms up in triumph, exhilaration pouring through him, but one wrong foot placement sent him crashing to the ground, throwing his arms out to catch himself instead.

Sprawled across the track, Jonah was breathing hard, taking stock of what hurt. Nothing was broken, as far as he could tell.

Kami rushed to his side and knelt over him. "Jonah, are you okay?"

Kids started crowding around her, each one looking at his running blade and then at him. But the final straw was when Coach Stubbs leaned down, his hands on his knees. "Are you all right, son?"

Humiliation pressed down on him. His worst nightmare had been falling in public and making a spectacle of himself and, here he was, flat on his back in front of his coach and the track team. He struggled to sit up, his shoulder protesting the movement. "I'm okay."

"Can you stand up?" Kami asked. "Let's get you over to the bench."

He did *not* want to stand up in front of them and embarrass himself any further. His knees and elbows were scraped, his ego was crushed, and the kids were looking at his running blade like it was an alien limb. He closed his eyes for a moment, wishing the crowd of people would disappear when he opened them. But they didn't.

With a deep breath, he carefully got on his knees and pushed himself up to a standing position. Getting his balance, he started to limp over to the bench. He sat down heavily and Kami started to sit down next to him, but he waved her away. "Go, do the practice with the kids, I'm fine."

His voice came out harsher than he intended and he saw a flash of hurt in Kami's eyes before she turned away. Jonah wanted to call her back, but she was already gone, calling out for the kids to start their warm-ups.

Coach Stubbs slipped into the seat next to him. "Any sprains or strains?" he asked, his voice business-like. Jonah was glad for that. He didn't want sympathy right now.

Jonah twisted to look at his elbow. "Nope, just scrapes." *And a bruised ego.* Some of the kids were still glancing his way and he ducked his head. He should have known he wasn't ready. All he wanted to do now was go home and curl up on the couch with Magnus. Watch some TV. Listen to music. Be alone.

Coach Stubbs leaned forward, his elbows on his knees. He didn't look at Jonah, his eyes on the students. "Jonah, you've got to get back out there. Don't let that fall be the end of it."

Jonah shook his head. "I'm not ready, Coach. That fall proves it."

"No, that fall proves you're out of practice. But I saw your face before you went down and you were remembering why you loved running. It was obvious your body was stretching back to those muscle memories. But you have a new muscle that needs extra work. That's why you've got to get back out there." He turned to look at Jonah, his eyes bright. "You've got it in you."

Jonah looked back out at the students who were starting to jog around the track. "Maybe another day when I can have the track to myself."

"Do you think those kids haven't fallen down? Felt like quitting?" He shook his head. "You can inspire them."

"I'm not anyone's inspiration, Coach," Jonah said, as he stood. "I'm just a guy trying to figure out his life."

"You could be more than that to these kids. You set records at this school in track and field and they look up to you. There's a chance to show them that a Hill Spring Warrior never gives up no matter what. You've got different challenges now, but this is your chance to start meeting them." The coach stood with him and adjusted the Hill Spring Warrior ball cap he always wore. "I'm not trying to pressure you, Jonah, but think about what I've said. You could help these kids. Or you could even do something like train for the Paralympics. Your runner's heart is still beating in there and just needs an outlet."

The coach's words charged through him, mixing fear with excitement. The coach had pushed him to his limits all through high school and helped him win races. But more than that, his coach had built character, focusing his team on goals that required willpower and perseverance, both things Jonah needed right now. He watched the coach exit the track, then started toward the locker room to change, waving to the kids who ran past him. He had a lot to think about.

Once he was back in his street clothes, he sat on the bottom bench of the bleachers and watched Kami work with the team. She was good at what she did and it was easy to see how much she cared about the kids. But could he ever be that confident again? Was running really in his future like the coach thought? He ran his hands through his hair. What would Kami think?

Practice was winding down and Kami jogged over to him as the kids were gathering up their stuff. "Hey," she said, her tone wary.

"Hey, yourself. Great practice." He stood and put his hands in his pockets. "Are you ready to go?" He cringed inwardly. It sounded like he couldn't wait to leave, but he didn't know what else to say. The humiliation of the fall had brought all his insecurities to the forefront again and he felt tongue-tied in front of her. Not to mention that the way he'd acted toward her afterward wasn't his proudest moment, but he didn't even know where to start to make things right with her.

They walked out to the car in silence and it didn't take long to get to Kami's house. "Thanks for coming," she said quietly before she got out of the car. "I hope you're okay."

He put his hand on her arm. "I'm sorry, Kami. For everything."

She gave him a sad smile and got out of the car. He watched her go inside before he closed his eyes. Why hadn't he told her what he was feeling? Talked it out?

He slowly drove home, thinking about all the things he should have said. He pulled into the driveway and took his time getting into the house. Magnus greeted him at the door, but didn't jump and merely licked his hands. The dog always seemed to know exactly what Jonah needed.

"Is that you, Jonah?" his mom called from the kitchen.

"Yeah," he said, walking down the hall to the family room.

Magnus waited until Jonah was safely sitting in his favorite chair in front of the fireplace, before he lay down at his feet. Jonah listened to his mom putter around in the kitchen. From the smell wafting through the house, she was baking again.

He sat and stared at the empty fireplace, remembering how he'd been sitting in this exact spot when Kami had knocked on his door in the snowstorm. The rest of that night had changed his life. Sitting with her in front of the fireplace, holding her in his arms. He'd felt happy. Whole. He wanted that feeling back again.

"Tell me about your day? Did you see Ben? Go to the track?" His mom offered him a spoon. "Want to help me drop the cookies on the pan?"

Jonah shifted in his seat and looked over at his mom. She meant well, but he really just wanted to be alone with his thoughts. "Ben was great." He looked down at Magnus and the dog perked up. "I think I'm going to take Magnus for a walk. He's been cooped up a lot lately."

His mom didn't seem to think anything of it. "All right. When you get back I should have some warm cookies ready."

Jonah stood and reached for the leash. "Sounds great. Thanks, Mom." He really was lucky to have her.

Magnus brushed his tail against Jonah's good leg and gave a little bark of excitement at the sight of the leash. Jonah put his coat and scarf on and walked back outside. Magnus took the lead as soon as they were on the sidewalk and pulled him to the left. Deciding to go with it, he followed and Magnus gave him a happy look, his tongue lolling out of his mouth with as close to a big doggie grin on his face as he could get.

After a few blocks, though, Jonah realized they were headed toward Kami's house. He started to pull back, when he saw Kami and Lola less than a block away. "Did you plan this, boy?" he asked, watching the two dogs' reactions when they spotted each other. They were definitely smitten.

His stomach tightened as he walked on, with Magnus straining at the leash for him to hurry. The closer he got, the easier it was to decide that he just needed to be honest with her. Frankly, he could use a sounding board with everything running through his mind. But first of all, he owed her one more really good apology.

He gave her a tentative smile to test the waters when she was close enough to hear him. "I think these two planned this little meeting."

Kami was aloof, giving him the professional smile she

probably gave all of the track team parents, but she hadn't kept walking, so maybe there was still a chance. She looked down at Lola who was nuzzling Magnus. "Who would have thought they'd be so sneaky?"

The dogs seemed unaware of their owners, wrapped up in sniffing each other. Jonah stepped closer to Kami and tentatively touched her forearm. "I owe you an apology."

She looked up at him, but didn't say anything, her blue eyes clouded with concern and uncertainty.

"One of my biggest fears was to fall in public and that happened today, but it was no excuse to speak to you harshly. I was embarrassed." He let his hand slide down her arm and enclosed her fingers in his. She didn't pull away. "Sometimes I let my fear of failure get the best of me."

She sighed. "Jonah, I understand, really. I was just worried you'd hurt yourself." Lola was pulling on her leash, ready to continue their walk, but Kami held her in place. "And you're not a failure. You never have been. Failure means you stop trying and that's not you."

"You know, you're even starting to sound like Coach Stubbs." He leaned forward just a bit, wanting to be closer, but not wanting to push. "He told me I needed to show my Hill Spring Warrior spirit."

Kami's mouth quirked up, as if she were trying to suppress a chuckle. "Yeah, I can totally picture him saying that. Let me guess, did he talk about your runner's heart?"

Jonah laughed at how well she could predict their old coach. "Yeah, he did, but in a way, he's right. I was feeling it before I fell."

"What else did you and the coach talk about?" Kami finally gave in to Lola's demands and they started walking slowly down the street, letting the dogs explore every new smell from one side of the sidewalk to the other.

Jonah was busy trying to hold her hand and manage Magnus who wanted to be as close to Lola as possible. "He talked about my future, actually. He thinks I can help the track team or train for the Paralympics. Running is in my blood and he saw how much I still loved it before I fell."

"What do you think? Is running in your future?" Kami tilted her head and looked over at him, curiosity in her eyes.

He took a breath, trying to imagine himself coaching or training. "Maybe. It would be a lot of work."

"You've never been afraid of work, though." She squeezed his hand. "Actually, I take that back. Now that I think about it, I remember your mom having to remind you pretty often when you had chores that needed to be done."

He met her gaze, glad the easiness between them had returned. "Okay, I admit that. But I've been better since I came home, just so you know." He sobered and watched the dogs play in the snow. "When I was on that track, for the first time in a long time, I felt free, as if my body had been waiting for me to run, prosthetic or not."

The dogs had wandered back to them, as if they knew something was happening. Putting his feelings into words was a little scary, but once it was out, Jonah knew they were true. He had loved it. The track, his heart and lungs, legs and arms, all working in harmony, had made him feel like he could do it.

"If running felt good, then I think you should definitely explore your options." Lola walked around Kami's feet and tangled them both in the leash. Looking down, Kami let go of Jonah's hand so she could step out of it.

"Wait." He pulled her back to him and Magnus joined Lola at their feet. "You know, I really like this idea of exploring my options, but let's talk about kissing options for a second," he said softly as he brushed her hair back from her face and leaned down, pressing his lips against her temple. "I could kiss you here." He let his lips trail down to her cheek. "Or here." He nuzzled the side of her neck, pressing kisses to her jawline.

Kami leaned her head back and let out a little gasp as he slowly worked his way toward her mouth. "Those are good options," she agreed, breathlessly. "But I like this option best." She quickly turned his face with her free hand and kissed him on the mouth.

Jonah smiled at her impatience, but it was his favorite option, too. As he explored her lips, his hand drifted down to her throat, his thumb gently resting over her pulse that was beating in time to his own. Their bond had been formed long ago and hadn't broken in the face of separation, as if the universe had linked them together, knowing what trials awaited and how much strength they could give each other when they reconnected again. When they were together, the future seemed less hazy, as if it were something bright instead of to be endured. With Kami, he felt invincible.

Tired of waiting for their owners, the dogs began barking excitedly, tangling their leashes around both Jonah and Kami.

She pulled back to look at Jonah's face. "We're going to fall," she warned, sizing up the snow bank next to them.

"I think I already did," he said as he pulled her close and kissed her once more.

Epilogue

Three months later

Kami was nervous. More for her students than for herself, but this was the first 10K race she'd run in a while, too. Making her way closer to the starting line, she found Jonah already there on the sidelines. He was holding two leashes and both him and the dogs looked happy at her approach.

"Is everything okay?" he asked, wrapping the leashes around one hand and reaching for her with the other.

"Yeah. How was work today?" Maybe if she took her mind off the race, her nerves would calm down.

"It was good. Mr. Branford is a good boss and loves numbers almost as much as I do. He assures me that there's room for me to move up from junior accountant and even a possibility of taking over for him someday." He shifted behind her so he could massage her neck with one hand.

"Are you sure you're not too tired after helping me move the last of my stuff into my new condo last night? I knew you should have gone home earlier."

"No, I'm not tired at all. Just hoping to at least place in this race." She bent her neck forward so he could get better access. "I wanted to see your new place. I've been thinking about looking around for an apartment of my own. Ben and Hailey are doing so well now, it's time to take the next step."

"You're an amazing sister and aunt, you know that?" He kissed her hair. "Maybe you could get a condo like mine. Ben liked it."

"Ben liked your big screen TV. He didn't want to go home."

"Which was my plan all along, of course." His voice was low in her ear. "If I can get Ben to want to stay a little longer, I know you will, too."

She smiled as her heart sped up at his touch. "I like your diabolical thinking." She turned in Jonah's arms. "My pre-race jitters aren't going away."

"You're going to do great. We've trained these kids well and they're ready." He took a second to get down on both knees to scratch Magnus's head. "Maybe you just need some dog therapy."

She got down next to him and put her arms around Lola's neck, giving her a loose hug. "Thanks, girl," she said, petting her. She scratched underneath Lola's chin and noticed a ribbon hanging from Lola's collar. "What's this?"

Looking over at Jonah, she drew her brows down. He was staring at her intently, with a funny look on his face. She pulled the ribbon off Lola's neck and held it up. A diamond solitaire was hanging from it.

"Oh, Jonah," she breathed. "It's beautiful." Her hands were shaking, but she managed to get the knot out and pull it free.

Jonah gently took it from her hands and moved a little closer until he was kneeling right in front of her. "The truth is, Kami, I've loved you for as long as I can remember. I lost sight of that for a little bit, but ever since you ended up at my door looking for your dog, I knew I couldn't ever let you go again. Will you marry me?"

She looked at this man who had made her heart feel whole from the moment he came into her life. Reaching out her arms, she hugged him to her. "Yes," she said. "Yes!"

He leaned in and kissed her. Applause erupted around them, but Kami couldn't hear anything except the barking dogs who were trying to give her their own kisses. She laughed and pulled back, quirking her eyebrow in question. Jonah understood immediately and nodded. They both opened their arms for the dogs, laughing as they got doggie congratulations with lots of slobbery kisses.

"Now Magnus and Lola will get their happily-ever-after, too," Jonah said, sliding the ring on Kami's finger.

"That seems fair, since they were the ones who helped us find each other again." She looked at the ring, sparkling in the sunlight, representative of so many hopes and dreams. Her heart could hardly contain her happiness.

"I love you," she said, putting her arms around his shoulders. "And guess what? My pre-race jitters are gone."

He gave her a sly grin. "My plan worked then. And I love you, too."

She reached up to rest her palm on his cheek, unable to resist kissing him again. Jonah had shown her what it meant to be loved and how it felt to share that strength with someone else. Whatever lay ahead, they would face it together, partners in every sense of the word.

How it had always been meant to be.

About The Author

Julie Coulter Bellon is an award-winning author of nearly two dozen published books. She loves to travel and her favorite cities she's visited so far are probably Athens, Paris, Ottawa, and London. She would love to visit Hawaii, Australia, Ireland, and Scotland someday. She also loves to read, write, teach, watch Hawaii Five-O, and eat Canadian chocolate. Not necessarily in that order.

Julie offers book reviews, book sales, writing and publishing tips, as well as her take on life on her blog http://ldswritermom.blogspot.com/ You can also find out about all her upcoming projects at her website www.juliebellon.com or you can follow her on Twitter @juliebellon